2. 50

Eddie's World

Eddie's World

CHARLIE STELLA

CARROLL & GRAF PUBLISHERS

NEW YORK

EDDIE'S WORLD

Carroll & Graf Publishers
An Imprint of Avalon Publishing Group Inc.
161 William St., 16th Floor
New York, NY 10038

Library of Congress Cataloging-in-Publication Data is available.

ISBN: 0-7867-0893-X

Printed in the United States of America
Distributed by Publishers Group West

Twenty-five years ago, in a creative writing class at Minot State College in North Dakota, a small school I attended on a football scholarship, I was forever hooked as a reader and wannabe writer of modern crime fiction.

It was the first day of class. Our instructor sat at his desk, glanced around the room at each of us, and creased open the paperback novel he was about to read from. He cleared his throat and leaned into the book:

"Jackie Brown, at twenty-six, with no expression on his face, said that he could get some guns."

It was the opening line from George V. Higgins' *The Friends of Eddie Coyle*.

The instructor, Dave Gresham, would become the single person I turned to over and over for support and inspiration as a writer. He is also a dear friend. I have been lucky to know him and his wonderful and talented family.

EDDIE'S WORLD is dedicated to Dave.

Others I am in great debt to include: my agent Bob Diforio; my three wonderfully bright and creative children (Nicole Hope, Charles Thomas and Dustin William); the memory of my father, Thomas Rocco Stella; several women who have put up with and survived me: Terry Stella (the mother of my children); Pat Rohe (the most successful and generous woman on the planet); Denise Stella (the smartest and sexiest woman on the planet), my mother, Hope (the greatest mommy on the planet), Gilda (the "Gilda-beast" — the greatest doggie on the planet); and the person for whom *EDDIE'S WORLD* was originally written (in a humble attempt to impress an impressive lady), a combination of all of the above, *Principessa*, Ann Marie Wood.

Other notes of thanks go to fellow writers: Robert Mladinich (whose first book, *From the Mouth of the Monster*, a magnificent and eerie probe into the mind of serial killer, Joel Rifkin, was released in November 2001), who's encouragement and advice during some stressful times was priceless, and Jaxon Ronin (J.R.), a talented screenwriter, who's dedication to his own work while I played solitaire (instead of writing myself), induced the necessary guilt to finish *EDDIE'S WORLD*.

More often than not, the federal witness protection program is a moral assault on our society. Deals with the Devil are evil by their nature. When people can trade up to nineteen lives for the opportunity to relocate from one coast to an Arizona desert (to ultimately establish a drug business), the government, whatever its original intent, has made fools of us all. Perhaps a more novel approach might be to rethink a Society Protection Program . . . where someone who admits to killing nineteen people might rot away in a cell before they burn in hell.

Pentiti, cangia vita:	*Repent, change your life:*
E l'ultimo momento!	*Your final moment has come!*

—Il Commendatore
(*Don Giovanni*)

Eddie's World

CHAPTER 1

THE TINY DINER ON THE LOWER EAST SIDE OF Manhattan was empty except for a heavyset man eating an omelet at the counter. The lone waitress, a tired redhead in her mid-thirties, leaned against the opening in the counter. The cook, somewhere in the back of the kitchen, was reading a newspaper.

Eddie Senta set a hand on the back of Tommy Gaetani's right shoulder as the two men filed down a narrow aisle with booths on either side. Eddie was a broad, stocky man with a thick neck. He had short, curly, black hair with streaks of gray, and a bright smile. He waited for the thinner Gaetani to slip into a booth before moving past his friend to sit across from him.

The two men signaled for coffee before the waitress made it to their table. Eddie was dressed in a light black windbreaker that he immediately took off. Tommy was wearing a heavy sweatshirt jacket and a wool cap. He removed the cap only.

"I didn't think I'd make it tonight," Tommy said. He rubbed at his thick mustache with one finger. "I got backed up on I95 outside Stamford. I thought I'd spend the rest of the night there."

"There aren't enough hours in a day," Eddie said. He folded his right leg up on the bench as he turned sideways in the booth. "I just did a shift for a law firm downtown. From noon to seven. They wanted me to stay but I wasn't in the mood. I can use a break from that shit."

The waitress brought two coffees and set them on the table. "Would you like to order dinner?" she asked.

Tommy looked to Eddie. "This place safe?"

Eddie winked at the waitress. "He's got a sensitive stomach."

The waitress smiled. "The special isn't bad. Stuffed peppers."

"Stuffed peppers it is," Tommy said.

"He's also a lot braver 'n I am," Eddie told the waitress. "Give me a cheeseburger deluxe."

The waitress wrote down the orders. Both men watched her ass as she walked away from them.

"To be young again," Tommy said.

Eddie stirred sugar into his coffee. "Tell me about it," he said. "I used to play football. I could run five miles a day, touch my palms flat on the floor. I can hardly make it up a flight of stairs anymore."

Tommy smiled as he sipped at his coffee. "I heard."

Eddie leaned back. "I didn't know it was common knowledge."

Tommy held his smile. "Although the guy I heard it from said it sounds a lot funnier coming from you."

"The guy you heard it from Nick Russo?"

"Uh-huh."

Eddie sipped his coffee. "He embellished it," he said as he set the cup down. "What happened was I was collecting for Joe Sharp, some guy went bust on him a few weeks earlier. Small change, four or five hundred. But the guy got under Joe Sharp's skin, you know what I mean? So he asks me to go to this joint on Fourteenth on the West Side. Ninth or Tenth Avenue someplace. Just off the corner. I find the super, ask about this guy I'm supposed to see, and he takes me on this adventure up five flights of stairs. It's a walk-up, for Christ sakes. I'm dying the entire time. I gotta stop at least two times on the way. I finally get to the top, and you know the guy isn't there. There's no way he's gonna be at the end of that journey. Not that I'm complaining, because let's face it, if the guy is there, he tells me to go and fuck myself, I'm not so sure I'm in a condition to do anything about it. Not after the five flights. Anyway, I'm leanin' against one of the crumbling walls in the hallway up there, huffing and puffing, trying to catch my breath."

Eddie exaggerated breathing hard as he continued the story.

"And I say to the super: 'You tell this guy ... the next time I see him ... I'll drag his ass ... down the block ... behind my car.'"

Both men laughed and sipped at their coffees. "P.S., you ever get the money?" Tommy asked.

"The guy dropped half of it off the next morning. I guess he figured I was serious, climbing all those stairs."

Both men paused to glance around the diner and then leaned in closer to each other across the table.

"When do you need the radio car?" Tommy asked.

"Couple days," Eddie said. "If I go through with it. I'm stuck in the hesitation waltz right now. The way things are, I mean, it's sometimes hard to pass on things like this. A guy blows smoke in your ear, you don't know it might turn into something. It looks attractive but it could just be smoke. I'm waiting for a vote of confidence. Something to tell me to go for it."

"Like a sign from God or something?"

Eddie shrugged. "Something like that."

"Because I do a mean Charlton Heston as Moses," Tommy said. "You ever see me do that one?" He sucked in some air, furrowed his eyebrows and spoke in a deep Charlton Heston-like voice. "I am the Lord thy God. Go for it."

"Heston played Moses," Eddie reminded him.

"How about a voice in the night then? Because if that's all you need, you got it right here. I'm not God or nothing. Let's face it; I'm a nobody.

But it is dark outside, and I do have a voice. I can sure use something right about now, if that counts for anything. I'm a guy in need of miracles. Trust me."

"Except I'm not really hurting right now," Eddie said. "Knock wood."

Both men knocked the top of the table with their fists.

"Not that I'm rich," he said. "Nothing like that. Between the computers and the street, I'm all right. My son just turned fifteen, so I'll always need a little something extra, but I'm okay, as money goes. Except there's something missing, you know what I mean? What it might or might not be is a mystery to me. Maybe a spark of life I need in my old age. Diane, when she isn't flaking off about some new Internet gimmick, she wants a kid. I can't even imagine one right now. So I know the spark isn't that, having a kid."

Tommy smiled. "How is Diane?"

Eddie rolled his eyes. "It's two years now we're married, and I still can't figure her out. Although she sure as shit thinks she's got me figured out."

"She still hate me?" Tommy was still smiling.

"Please. It's not you she hates. It's us, what we are."

"Wannabes? Because she should know better than that by now. Especially living with you."

"She thinks we're out of touch," Eddie said. "At least I think that's what it is. I won't see a therapist, so that disqualifies me from being in touch. You know how that goes."

Tommy mimicked chatter with his right hand. "Women like to talk about their problems. Whatta you gonna do?"

"Hey, we only knew each other a couple months when we got married," Eddie said. "We both thought it was the right thing to do, you know. Like it was magic or something, I don't know. We got along. I liked her flakiness. I know she was intrigued with me, with us, what we do. Brother, did that rub off fast. Now she wants a kid. Her eyes get wet every time she sees one. Scares the shit out of me."

"I know the feeling," Tommy said. "My old lady sees a kid, her eyes get all fucking big, and I want to catch a flight across the country. They just don't get it, some broads. At least now, though, the hole I'm in with money, Val knows enough not to bring it up."

Eddie creased his napkin in quarters. "So, I'm searching, Tommy. You know what I mean? I'm searching for something."

Tommy laughed. "Something deep, right?"

Eddie continued folding the napkin. "The meaning of fucking life."

Tommy offered a cigarette. "You find it, let me know," he said.

Eddie signaled the waitress and held up the cigarette, mutely asking for permission to smoke. The waitress glanced around the diner and shrugged one shoulder.

"There's nobody here to complain," she said.

Both men lit up.

"Or a score," Tommy said. "Maybe it's that you're looking for."

Eddie nodded. "What I've been thinking, yeah."

"I hear what you're saying," Tommy said. "Except I'm in no position to choose right now. At least you got that other thing with the computers. I'm sweating this dry spell out cold turkey. Nothing but crumbs falling around me. Nothing serious. Few bucks here, and another few there, but not enough to make a difference. I'm late two months inna row on the mortgage, and I'm not so sure I'm gonna make it next month. I got less than ten grand out on the street and at least half of that is delinquent. Why I was in Stamford this afternoon, chasing another deadbeat. So, whatever you need this radio car for, consider me in. It's a guy owes me anyway. The guy with the car. I lent him the ten grand he needed to buy the radio. He owes me, so the car's a freebee. And I can use whatever score you got. Computers, cash, cigarettes, nylons, or bloody fuckin' tampons. Beggars can't be choosers."

"Diane thinks it's a midlife crisis," Eddie said. "At least that's what her therapist tells her. I can hardly tell anymore who's doing the talking, whether it's Diane or her therapist."

"Maybe it is a midlife crisis," Tommy said. "I admire you for having one. Guy like me, in the shape I'm in now, I can't afford to have a midlife crisis."

Eddie took a drag on his cigarette. "If that's what it is, I hope I get over it soon."

Tommy set his cup down on the table and touched the edges of his mustache with his fingertips. "So, what are we talking about, if you don't mind my asking?"

The waitress brought a basket of sliced Challa bread to the table. Eddie took a slice and buttered it. Tommy bit into a slice without any butter.

"Your food should be ready in a few minutes," the waitress said to Eddie. "More coffee?"

Eddie smiled. "Thanks."

Both men waited for their second cup of coffee to be poured before resuming their conversation.

"We'll take a ride near the place after we eat," Eddie said. "You'll let me know what you think. Maybe spot something I don't see. I've been led to believe in a great expectation on this one. But you know the prob-lems with that, right? One man's great is another man's pittance. That's my problem. I'm confused about where I am on this. Is it something great I want or just another pittance?"

"Well, a pittance is still more 'n what I got going right now," Tommy said. "So, whatever it is, I'm in. I can have the car on a day's notice. We're going to see the place tonight, that'll just get me more excited. Just to have an iron in the fire gives me a woody these days. I don't know if blue balls have anything to do with a midlife crisis, but mine turned purple like six months ago. I don't find something out there to make payments with, I get the feeling I can start contemplating alimony along with the child support I'm already late on."

Eddie smiled. "We'll make something happen. Let's eat and then go take a look-see."

The waitress brought both dinners and set them on the table. She grabbed a full bottle of ketchup from the next table and handed it to Eddie.

"Thanks, hon," Eddie said.

The waitress offered him a wink. "Sure," she said. "My pleasure."

Tommy caught the action between Eddie and the waitress. "I'd take that as a vote of confidence."

Eddie nodded. "Yeah," he said. "Maybe it was."

CHAPTER 2

TWENTY MINUTES AFTER FINISHING THEIR DINNERS, Tommy and Eddie were cruising Lexington Avenue in Eddie's Saab. Traffic was heavy but moving. Eddie parked on the northeast corner of Lexington Avenue off Thirty-third Street. Both men lit cigarettes.

Eddie pointed across the avenue up the hill that was Thirty-third Street. "Up there," he said. "On the southeast corner of Park. It's a residential building with a couple floors of office space. The residential lobby is in the middle of the block, next to the Citibank there. Our spot is on the other side of the building, on Thirty-second Street, on the third floor. There's one elevator stops at the second and third floors. There's a medical office takes up all of two and most of three."

"So there won't be anybody up there," Tommy said. "That's good."

"Nobody should be, that's for sure. The place has got about fifteen computers, in case the other thing don't go down. It's supposed to be there. If it is, we're in and out with whatever else we can carry. Laptops, I figure. Whatever we don't have to go back for."

"What's the other thing?" Tommy asked.

"Cash," Eddie said. "Fifteen, maybe twenty thousand. Like I said, we find that, maybe we forget the computers altogether, except to make it look like a kid-type thing. Break in and run."

Tommy was smiling. "The thought of that kind of scratch right now is enough for me. It would go a long way to taking care of some things."

"Except we're working in thirds," Eddie said. "So, if it's there, fifteen large, or however much we find, it gets broke down to thirds."

"Who's the other third?"

"Person getting us inside. The same one brought this to me."

"I get the feeling I shouldn't ask anymore," Tommy said. "Which is fine with me. Five grand would do more than enough for me right now. And I don't see any other way of coming across it, other than walking into a bank with a note and a water pistol."

"What the hell," Eddie said. "I worked here about six months ago. Temping. Word Processing. I know the layout. I know the building. Somebody inside is a friend. She gave me the thing."

"A she?" Tommy asked. "She givin' you anything else?"

Eddie adjusted his rearview mirror to watch for cop cars cruising the area. "Please, I got enough problems at home with Diane. She wants space and a kid. I mention that? She's thinking of having and raising a kid alone. Smart as she is, sometimes Diane has a clear fucking head. No, it's nothing like that with this woman from the office. I met her through the job. The day I left, I forgot my CD player I use when I'm working and I went back for it after hours. I walk in on her and the guy owns the joint. I heard moans and shrieks from this office across from where I left my CD player. Who knew what was going on in there? I heard her yelp-like, and I opened the door. The prick was jackhammering her ass. He pulled out, blood all over the end of his dick, and he yelled at me, "the fuck you doing here"?

I looked at Sarah, the woman, make sure it wasn't rape, and she waved me off, all red-faced. I asked anyway, you all right? The guy screams at me again, and I tell him to shut the fuck up or I'll turn him around and bleed him the same way. She waved me away again so I figure it was consensual. I went and got my CD player and that was that. Pretty freaky, huh?"

Tommy made a face.

"Exactly. I had some vivid fucking dreams from that image for a long time afterward. Then she calls me up later that same night through the agency I worked for. Tells me how sorry she was, that she wants to buy me lunch the next week. I was more concerned about her, if she wasn't damaged and all. She's all fucked up and wants to explain to me how the prick she works for told her I can't temp there anymore, duh, and would I please meet with her. Don't ask me why, but I said yes. I wind up feeling sorry for her. She's a sad story."

"Not if it was consensual."

"There's more to it. I find out she's a boozer. You know, in and out of the program. In and out of work, too. The guy there, her boss the prick, he lets her come back whenever she's out on binges and benders. She gives him some extra attention, and he keeps her employed."

Tommy shook his head. "Sorry, I still don't make her a saint for that."

"I know, I know," Eddie said. "Except she really is one of life's losers. Bad relationships, bad luck. Whatever. She's had a lot of dirt shoveled on her, one way or another. The booze, I guess, is what people like that do. They numb themselves."

Tommy shrugged. "She's your friend. I still don't see why she'd give you this kind of a score, fifteen grand, and only ask for a third. Especially when she's the insider. First thing they're gonna do, the cops, is look on the inside."

"The prick had her service one of his friends he does business with," Eddie continued. "The guy got physical with her, banged her around. The prick she works for slips her an extra couple hundred and gives her a few days off for compensation. I found out and managed to get the name of the guy from her, the one banged her around. I waited a couple months and took Jimmy Mangino with me."

Tommy's head snapped back. "Jimmy bench-press?"

Eddie nodded. "The same. The girl beater was on crutches shortly thereafter. I saw Jimmy do it. Broke the fucker's legs without the use of a bat. Anybody ever asks, you think Jimmy Mangino is tough? Tell them you're fuckin-A right you do."

"And he keeps a good secret," Tommy said. "I never heard a word about this. Nobody I know heard of it. And he went up, what, five, six weeks ago?"

"For heavy shit. I let him take the guy's Rolex. I'll bet he was wearing it, too, when he was brought in on that other thing."

"Jimmy liked the phones, too," Tommy said. "He probably bet and lost that Rolex before he had the chance to set the time."

Eddie took one last drag on his cigarette and tossed it out of the car. "Anyway, my friend has it in for the prick she works for. Hearing this stuff, you can't blame her. I think she's tough and smart enough to keep her mouth shut once they find the place was robbed. All they can do is accuse her. Fire her probably, but she's fine with that. She says she wants out anyway. Her counselor wants her out. Says it's a vicious cycle she keeps herself in, doing whatever this prick wants just to keep a job she can get anywhere."

"It's your call, Eddie," Tommy said. "I'm just along for the ride. You say it's thirds, it's thirds."

"If this thing works out, we go in and take what we came for, and we're both up a nice piece of change," Eddie said. "Otherwise we take the computers. We go this weekend because the night-cleaning crews don't come back to work until Monday. Sometimes they have that weird shift when Thursday is Friday, but not in this building. At least that's what I was told. Shouldn't be anybody up there, say, three o'clock in the morning."

"Sounds good to me," Tommy said. "Could be the break you need. Use the money from this thing to take a break from the computers."

"Could be. The days keep rolling into one another, you know what I mean? Monday is Tuesday is Wednesday. Between the computers and collecting and fighting with Diane, I blink and the weekend has come and gone and the bullshit starts all over again."

Tommy played with his mustache. "Twenty-four hours, seven days a week. I hear you. Except you should try owing all the time. Then the twenty-four/sevens, they start to feel like a fucking avalanche waiting to happen. That's what it's like for me. One big fucking wait for the next financial disaster to pancake me."

"Sounds like we both need a break," Eddie said.

Tommy leaned to his left. "There's nobody up there the weekend, I say we go."

"Which is why I want to go with a radio car, you can get it from the guy owes you. We both get dressed so it looks like we're two Joes stopped back at the office to pick something up. The cops won't give us a second look, they see a corporate Lincoln Town Car. We go up to the office, we do our thing, and we come back down. We load the trunk fast and drive the fuck away. Two office Joes had a late night, brought their work home for the weekend."

"I like it," Tommy said. "I like it a lot. You're right, the cops won't think twice, they see a radio car parked out front."

"You're sure about the radio car, right?" Eddie asked.

Tommy nodded. "I'll get it first thing in the morning. The guy won't mind. He's backed up, what he owes me."

"Good enough."

"I'm assuming we have access to the office. Alarms, keys, and so on."

"Done and done."

Tommy slapped Eddie on the arm. "So, all this for the sake of some broad you feel sorry for?"

Eddie held up a finger. "And the money. Don't forget the money."

"Who could forget that?"

Both men lit fresh cigarettes.

Tommy leaned back. "I'll tell you one thing, my friend. You lead an interesting life."

Eddie laughed. "Or a confused one. Depends you see a therapist or not."

"No thanks. I got enough problems I already know about."

"It doesn't matter, you know about them," Eddie said. "They'll just claim you're ignoring your problems, you ever admit to them. It's a fail-safe system these clowns have." He counted on his fingers. "We're all nuts, every one of us. Two, we're all in denial about something. And three, none of us will ever be cured."

"At a hundred bucks a pop," Tommy said.

Eddie toasted Tommy with his cigarette. "Salute."

"Well, at least you can exist in two worlds. I tip my hat to you. At least you got that going for you."

"And maybe I can't fit into one or the other," Eddie said. "I can't give up the street stuff and do what my wife wants, which is to play ball with the office world, get a steady computer job, and take the Long Island Railroad every morning. And I can't see myself running coffee errands for wiseguys I don't respect. What's that, like lost in the middle someplace? Definitely lost."

Tommy pointed at Eddie. "Don't knock it. You still have choices. That's a lot more than the rest of us have."

Eddie waved that off. "Yeah, well, if I want smoke blown up my ass, I'll go to Diane's therapist."

Tommy slapped Eddie's arm again. "You're still my hero."

"What I am, Tommy, at least sometimes, is one big sucker."

"Some people like to know the difference. Between a hero and a sucker."

Eddie started the car. "You know what I think?" he asked, after the engine had settled and was idling. "In the end, I mean? There is no difference. None whatsoever."

CHAPTER 3

James Singleton smiled at a naked Sarah Parker from her queen-size bed. She stood, bent at the waist, in the dim light of the hallway outside of her bedroom, combing her long blonde hair. She was in fair shape for a forty-one-year-old alcoholic. Her body still had enough curves and big enough breasts to attract most men. When she stood up straight, the bedroom light shone brightly on her face, which showed the wear and tear of a rough life. She squinted as she turned away from the light.

They had just finished having sex for the second time since they left a bar on Third Avenue. Sarah had jammed tissue paper inside of her vagina to keep from leaking Singleton's semen. Singleton liked the sight of his new girlfriend standing there with the tissue visible amidst her blonde pubic hairs. He looked to his left and saw his own image in the mirror above Sarah's dresser. Singleton waved Sarah toward him so that he could see both of them in the same reflection.

"Not again," Sarah said, walking over to him.

Singleton smiled. He was a tall, muscular black man with a thick scar running from his left collarbone up his neck to his chin. He was thirty-three years of age and only two weeks out of Fishkill State Penitentiary. The scar was the result of a slashing that Singleton received in prison. The wound, made by a weapon fashioned from fused pieces of jagged metal, had nearly killed him. As Singleton looked at Sarah's legs and ass in the mirror, he ran two fingers along the length of his scar, starting from under his chin.

"I think that's sexy," Sarah said. She leaned over to trace Singleton's fingers against the scar.

"You should've seen the other guy," Singleton said.

They had met two days ago. Singleton was in a bar he was about to rob when he spotted the worn-looking blonde with the big chest. Sarah had bought him a few drinks, told him a story about being a recovering alcoholic, and thanked him for keeping her from drinking. A few cigarettes later, she had taken him home to fuck.

Now she was letting him stay the night again. Singleton was getting used to her hospitality. The woman had nothing else in her life. Somehow, being around him was keeping her from drinking. She was paying his way, providing him with food and drink, and putting out in the meantime. All for the sake of company, as far as Singleton could figure.

He reached out to run his big right hand around the curve of her hip, but Sarah pulled back.

"I think I'm too sore for anything else down there tonight," she told him.

Singleton flexed his muscles. "Superman," he said. "The white prize has begged for mercy."

Sarah sat on the bed alongside Singleton. She took his hand. "I don't know how much of a prize I am, but I am asking for mercy for a while."

Singleton kissed her hand. "You got it," he said.

"You really have to leave tonight?" she asked him.

"Got to," Singleton said. "Got to see a man about something I'm gonna need for your friend with all the gold." He made a pretend gun out of his right hand.

Sarah frowned. "I wish you didn't have to get one of those," she said.

"It just for show," he said, waving his fake gun. "About as useful as this."

Sarah rubbed at her temples.

"I'm no killer, baby," Singleton continued. "This thing I'm getting is just to scare the man, he gets any crazy ideas in his head."

"Wait until you see this guy," Sarah said. "He'll probably need Pampers from shitting his pants. He's no tough guy. He's a crooked jeweler from New York who relocated to the Caribbean because he could take advantage of tourists down there with less competition than up here. He's a worm. He won't give you any trouble."

Singleton touched the tip of Sarah's nose. "And sometimes it's those guys who carry the little piece you can't see through the clothes. Sometimes they the ones put a bullet in you, you not watching."

Sarah frowned again. "I guess," she said. "Just be careful. I'm afraid this is getting out of hand. It's supposed to be a simple thing. Now that there's a gun involved. . . ."

Singleton softly brushed Sarah's cheek with his right hand. "Ta-ta-ta-ta," he said. "Everything will go fine. This is nothing but butter. The gun is just something to keep things from getting out of control. This boy's not interested in things getting crazy, baby. Businessman sees a gun, he do his thing, which is business. Trust me."

Sarah laid her head on Singleton's stomach. "I still wish you didn't have to go tonight," she said.

"I still wish you let me go after the cash," Singleton said. "Lot easier to work with than gold. Beside the fact you get dollar for dollar. Fifteen thousand in gold is worth less than half when the man sees a black man come to fence it."

"Which would be more than five thousand dollars," Sarah said.

"Which is a small fortune right now. To both of us. You and me. And don't forget the cash. I'm getting some of that, too."

"Except for all the work," Singleton said. "Not to mention the risk. Lot easier what you got your friend doing for you, speaking of the cash. Go into an empty office the middle of the night, take a bundle of money and walk out."

Sarah looked up from Singleton's stomach. "He's taking risks, too," she said. "And I know he doesn't need the money. He's doing this for me."

Singleton flashed Sarah an exaggerated wink. "Yeah and maybe he bigger than me down there?" he said.

Sarah shot Singleton an exaggerated frown. "I wouldn't know," she said. "But I owe it to him, the cash end of this. And I brought it to him before I even met you. Eddie has done a lot for me. I told you that. I can't change up on him now. Especially since he doesn't know about you or that I'm going after the gold. He thinks it's just the cash I'm after."

"And just keep it that way," Singleton said seriously. "The man hears I'm on parole or somethin', he might go and ruin a beautiful thing here. Then I have to go look for him someday."

"Don't talk like that," Sarah said.

Singleton smiled at her. "That's all it is," he said. "Just talk."

Sarah lightly kissed Singleton's stomach. "I just don't want anything to go wrong," she said. "I've had bad luck all my life. All my relationships go bad sooner or later. I guess I'd like for this one to wait until later." She kissed his stomach again. "And I don't want you to get into trouble again. Now that I told you about the gold, I mean. I have nothing against this guy selling the gold to my boss. He's a worm and all, but he's never done anything to me. It's my boss I'd like revenge against."

Singleton shrugged. "It just a wish, baby, the cash. We can work with cash pronto. The gold we gonna have to hold onto awhile. And if the man's a worm, he's a worm. Don't go getting soft on worms now. He got dirty gold, there's a reason for it."

"I guess," Sarah said.

"And it's no big deal, you feel you owe your friend, this Eddie guy. We do whatever you want. I like for this to last myself, you and me."

Sarah kissed his stomach one more time. "Maybe we can get away for a long weekend someplace," she said. "I can borrow on my credit card or something. As soon as this thing is over."

Singleton guided her head down his stomach. "Maybe you can take care of business, leave me the four hundred I'm gonna need for later, take a long nap. Get some sleep and recover so a man can get back to work again in the morning."

Sarah looked up at Singleton with a smile. She was holding his erect penis in her right hand. "You call that work, what you do to me? I'm the one has to handle this thing."

Singleton placed both hands behind his head as he relaxed and closed his eyes. "Feel free to go ahead and handle it," he said.

* * * * *

Forty-five minutes later, James Singleton was standing in a vestibule of a Harlem project building on One-Hundred Twenty-third Street. A young Puerto Rican man wearing a black skullcap handed Singleton a heavy brown paper bag.

"You get a three-eighty?" Singleton asked.

The Puerto Rican nodded.

"It feels heavier," Singleton said.

"That the extra clip," the Puerto Rican said. "You asked for an extra clip. They tied with rubber bands."

Singleton dead-eyed the Puerto Rican. Four years earlier, on the eve of his twenty-ninth birthday, Singleton had bought a weapon from the same dealer just a few blocks north of the same Harlem project. It had been a Smith & Wesson .9mm. It was one of a dozen handguns stolen from a Long Island sporting goods store only a week before.

Although he hadn't planned to kill back then, Singleton had used the Smith & Wesson to commit his first murder. He had stalked a drunken man in a business suit from a midtown bar to an automatic teller machine on Twenty-third Street. Singleton had watched the drunken man from a dark doorway directly across the street. The drunk had staggered inside the ATM station, withdrew some money, and then staggered back out. He was just hailing a taxi when Singleton started across the street. Then another mugger that Singleton had not seen got there first. The mugger poked the drunk in the ribs, and the drunk handed him his wallet. Singleton yelled at the mugger to freeze. When the mugger started to run, Singleton shot him twice in the back.

Ten minutes later, riding in the back of a taxi, Singleton found out that he'd committed murder for two wrinkled tens and four fresh twenties.

Now Singleton jammed the paper bag inside of his pants under his jacket. "This thing used the last few nights?" he asked.

The Puerto Rican looked around. "It's what the man had for two-fifty," he said. "You want something clean, you got to have the cash. Personally, I take the thing out back and try it, make sure it works, before I take off. No refunds after that."

"On you?" Singleton asked. "Should I try it on you?"

The Puerto Rican held up both his hands. "Chill, bro," he said. "You asked me to see what I could do and I did it. I can ask but I doubt they gonna lease you one. You want to shop, be my guest. Neighborhood's chock full of stash. You leave now, though, the price goes up. Two-fifty will be three half an hour from now. Four in an hour. Four-fifty in an hour and a half. And so on."

Singleton frowned as he paid the man the balance of the cost of the weapon. "You ever see me before?" he asked.

The Puerto Rican squinted. "See who?"

"You know me?" Singleton asked.

The man closed his eyes. "Know who?"

CHAPTER 4

EDDIE AND DIANE SENTA HAD JUST STARTED THEIR third year of marriage. Both had been married before. Eddie had one child from a previous marriage; Diane had none.

Diane was a striking woman, tall, lean, and muscular from years of aerobics and weight training. Although she was a chain-smoker, she was also a runner. Her hobby was cyber voyeurism.

A senior marketing executive, she had recently signed on with a California Internet company that was experimenting with on-line marketing research. It was one of the few such companies to survive the economic decline of 2000 and 2001. She was given stock options, a healthy salary, and benefits and was assigned to run the New York City office.

Since her marriage to Eddie, Diane's career had taken off. She had earned six-figures before signing with the new company. Now, her potential income from stock options alone could make her a millionaire in a few years.

Because of her new situation, Diane wanted some personal changes in her life. Between her ticking biological clock and her therapist,

Diane believed that she wanted a child and further that she should raise it alone. Eddie wasn't interested in having another child. He was more concerned with the changes in Diane's life that were affecting their marriage. Lately, they seemed to argue about everything.

When Eddie returned home after his meeting with Tommy, Diane was waiting up for him. She was chain-smoking Merit Ultra-lights. The television was on, but the sound was off. She waited until Eddie was finished in the bathroom before turning on the bedroom lights.

"Uh-oh," Eddie said, when the lights went on.

"It's two o'clock in the morning," Diane said.

Eddie didn't look at his wife. "I had things to do," he said. He started taking his clothes off on his side of the bed. He dropped them, item by item, onto the rug. He could feel Diane's stare. He glanced at her and frowned.

"Your son called," Diane said. "I left you a note."

"I saw it."

"You're supposed to see him tomorrow."

Eddie sat on the bed and pulled the covers down. "I'll try," he said. "I don't know if I can tomorrow." He saw the clothes that he had left on the floor and picked them up.

He had been educated in two distinct but related worlds. His mother was an organized and educated woman. His father was a rough blue-collar man of the street. Whereas his mother had tried to protect him by forcing him to read at a young age, his father had pushed him out of the house and taught him to fight his own battles. Eddie had learned balance at an early age and mastered it as an adult. He resisted impulses to drift too far one way or the other.

Married life was something Eddie couldn't resist. It was a part of the culture that he had grown up with. It was the security that middle-class men sought. Diane seemed to be in search of a pedigree that Eddie didn't possess. He was growing tired of defending himself about it.

"Things aren't right," Diane said. Eddie crossed the room to drop the clothes in the hamper. On his way back, Diane said, "We have to talk."

Eddie sat on the bed again. "Yeah, I figured," he said. "You're waiting up. That usually means you want to talk about something."

"You don't make it easy."

"Because I'm home late? I'm home late a lot. I work nights. What's the big deal?"

"No big deal at all, so long as I'm content to cyberfuck strange men over the Internet and get myself off," Diane said.

"Do you have to talk like that?"

"How do you want me to talk?"

Eddie made a face. "A little more delicate," he said. "Not like some porno star."

Diane rolled her eyes. "Please," she said.

Eddie lit a cigarette. "What is it you want, Diane?" he asked.

"I want a baby," she said.

"Here we go."

"I'm serious."

"I'm sure you are."

"I want a baby."

Eddie shook his head as he shrugged. "I can't," he said. "I don't want another kid now. You know that."

Diane was clenching her teeth. "And I do want one, damn you!"

"Yeah, well, go and have one."

"Thank you," she said sarcastically. "In the meantime, I think I found a donor."

"Fine," Eddie said and then started to laugh. "What's his screen name?"

"Very funny."

Eddie suppressed his laughter. "Sorry."

Diane took a few long drags on her cigarette. "The donor is my new boss out in California," she finally said.

Eddie's face tightened.

"I thought that would get your attention," Diane said. "It's just for the genetics. I'm not having an affair. I'm not in love with him. It's about having a baby. He's a marathon runner and a Ph.D."

Eddie rubbed his face. "Did you do it already?" he asked. "You and the Ph.D."

"Of course not," Diane said. "He's the one I picked. I haven't done anything yet. That's why I want to talk with you."

"I guess I should feel fuckin' honored, you want to discuss it with me first, fucking some other guy?"

"There's no need to be sarcastic."

"Of course not. I'm out doing business, taking risks, and you're on the Internet picking genetic matches to have a kid with. Jesus Christ, Diane. Give me a fucking break here."

"I want to raise it alone," she said. "By myself."

Eddie was trying to maintain his composure. "Fine," he said. "I figured we're headed this way sooner or later. Now's as good a time as any."

"But I'm not sure I want you out of my life," Diane added.

"Excuse me?"

"I'm not sure I want you out of my life. My child will need a father figure. And it's not like I hate you, Eddie. It's not like we're not good together."

Eddie shook his head. "What the fuck are you talking about?" he asked.

"Except for this shit you still do," Diane went on. "With Tommy Gaetani and Joe Sharpetti and the rest of your mob friends. You're a good man, Eddie. You're just confused. You're going through a midlife crisis, and you aren't trained enough to handle it."

"You got that figured out, huh?"

"More or less, yes."

"More or less, my ass."

"Anyway, the way I see it, I can have my child over the next year or so, raise it the first six months by myself, settle in somewhere, and then you can come back into my life. Our life. The baby's and mine. You wouldn't have to move in."

Eddie smiled. "And what if I'm not interested? This is a nice fantasy you're having here, Diane. You haven't lost your sense of fucking humor or imagination, that's for sure." He took a drag from his cigarette. "But while you're at it, deciding my future for me, why don't you consider having one of your cyber psychoboyfriends be the daddy? Let one of them play father of the year to this idea of yours because to tell you the truth, I don't think I'm interested. I have my own kid I don't see enough already, in case you forgot. The one called here tonight? I feel guilty enough about Jack to not want to do the same thing, not be there, to another kid."

Diane pointed at Eddie. She was about to interrupt when he cut her off.

"No, I'm serious," Eddie said. "There isn't a night I don't go to bed with this private fucking prayer in my head, and I'm not a religious man, Diane. It's a prayer born of guilt. A prayer just in case there really is somebody listening who can do something."

Diane folded her arms across her chest. Eddie took a moment.

"Do you know what I say every night once I close my eyes?" he asked his wife. "Do you have any idea? I say, please God, if anything bad has to happen, please let it be to me. Leave my son alone. Let it be me. Let it be me. Let it be me. Three fucking times I have to say that to myself, let it be me, before I can even consider trying to sleep. What that is, what that has become, is a fuckin' compulsive disorder I have now, that I gotta say that to myself every fucking time I try and go to sleep. Because the guilt I feel is real. Because I'm not there, anything bad happens. Can you understand that?"

"I never said you shouldn't see your son," Diane said.

"It's not about what you say," Eddie said. "It's about what I feel."

Diane was about to speak when Eddie cut her off again. "Look, this was fun for a while, okay. When we first met, the first year or two we were married. It's probably the same for you with me. You were intrigued by the street stuff when we first met. But it got old, right? Same here, this routine of yours, this never-ending freaky shit you pull, it's old. I enjoyed your flaky side for a while. Now, I'm sorry to say, I think the novelty is worn off."

Diane took a few drags on her cigarette. "This is all about control, isn't it?" she asked.

"Jesus Christ," Eddie said in frustration. "You should hear yourself. You're fucking scary is what you are."

"I'm sorry if I don't want a live-in gangster father figure for my child, Eddie. Excuse me, a confused live-in gangster father figure. Because I know you're still not sure about what you want to do with the rest of your life. I know you're not really into that other shit, or you would have gone the entire route and taken your gangster oath already."

Eddie rolled his eyes. "My midlife crisis, you told me."

"Well, that's what it is," Diane said. "Only you're not in touch enough to deal with it."

"But I'm in touch enough so you want me to be the daddy. What did you say? How long was it, six months after you give birth? I think you're not in touch with reality, Diane. That's what I think. You spend too much time with your shrink and on the Internet."

"I'm acting out my fantasies on the Internet," Diane said. "Better there than in real life. Or would you prefer I have sex with another man? Or two men? Or partake in an orgy?"

Eddie squinted at her. "Is that what you do on that thing?"

Diane frowned. Eddie threw his hands up in frustration as he turned away from her. "And I'm the one with the crisis?"

"Yes, you are!" Diane yelled, stomping the floor until he was attentive again. "I'm dealing with my crisis. The Internet is probably the only thing saving this marriage."

"Except you found a donor, right?" Eddie asked. "Wasn't that what started this, this sick conversation? You want to tell me that you want to fuck your new boss in California because he runs marathons and he's a Ph.D. Very nice. I'm happy for you." He rubbed his face again.

Earlier, Diane had been drinking wine in bed. She poured herself a fresh glass. Eddie lay flat on the bed and covered his face with a pillow.

"I'm also angry because of where you've been tonight," Diane said. "Your shift ended long before you came home, Eddie. And you collect on weekends. Which means you were out with Tommy or another one of those guys, and nothing good ever comes of that."

"Good night, Diane," Eddie said from underneath his pillow. "I'm going to sleep now."

"Of course you are," Diane said.

"Good night," Eddie grumbled.

CHAPTER 5

THEY HAD MET AT *CHRISTINA'S* RESTAURANT WHERE Eddie often ate dinner. Diane was with two girlfriends from work and Eddie was eating dinner at the bar. They had noticed each other when Diane stopped at the bar for a cigarette. Eddie gave her a light and complimented her business suit. Diane returned the interest and bought Eddie a drink. Later, they exchanged telephone numbers.

They started dating almost immediately. Diane had just left her first husband. Eddie had just divorced his first wife after nearly seven years of marriage. Both had outgrown their partners, and each was anxious for something new.

Within a month, they started living together. They were married three months later. Their troubles started during their second year of marriage. The flakiness that had originally attracted Eddie to Diane had become too unpredictable. The excitement of Eddie's world had become too dangerous for Diane.

When she decided she wanted children, Diane required her husband to settle down in a way that he found emasculating.

Now they were at the crisis point of their marriage. Diane needed

Eddie to compromise on the bigger issues. Eddie needed to keep his world from shrinking.

Diane couldn't sleep thinking about it. So she went on-line as her screen name, BeigeThong, and teased male screen names with tales of a cheating wife. She role-played a threesome with two screen names and an orgy with a half dozen others, and then changed to a long, involved tease session with a screen name, BLKHOSE4WW, that belonged to someone who claimed to be a black fireman searching for white women.

At the end of her tease session, after BLKHOSE4WW claimed that he had ejaculated all over his keyboard, Diane received an instant message from Mike Linton, her new boss and the man she was expecting to impregnate her.

LINTON:	"I'm checking e-mails. What are you doing on-line at this time?"
DIANE:	"Teasing dirty men like yourself."
LINTON:	"Feel free to tease away."
DIANE:	"I have a headache."
LINTON:	"LOL. You stopping bye tomorrow?"
DIANE:	"So far, I am. If not tomorrow, one day this week."
LINTON:	"I'm looking forward to it."
DIANE:	"I brought you up with Eddie tonight."
LINTON:	"Uh-oh."
DIANE:	"He didn't appreciate it."
LINTON:	"Neither do I."
DIANE:	"He thinks I'm crazy."
LINTON:	"What did you tell him?"
DIANE:	"My husband isn't interested in making his wife pregnant."
LINTON:	"What did you say?"
DIANE:	"I told him I found a donor."

LINTON: "He's your husband. You shouldn't taunt him."

DIANE: "We discussed ending that, too. The husband-wife thing."

LINTON: "I can understand that."

DIANE: "I think he was jealous."

LINTON: "How much did you tell him?"

DIANE: "About your Ph.D. and the running."

LINTON: "I really wish you hadn't."

DIANE: "It makes him crazy that I chose somebody. He thought I was making it all up."

LINTON: "Great. Should I leave town tonight?"

DIANE: "He was such a cynic. He didn't think there would be anybody like you out there."

LINTON: "It's the details that can agitate a man, Diane."

DIANE: "It's a genetic choice, Mike. He'll just have to live with it."

LINTON: "You didn't tell him you were coming here tomorrow, I hope?"

DIANE: "Of course not."

LINTON: "Good, don't."

DIANE: "I would never tell him something like that."

LINTON: "There are some things one shouldn't be honest and up front about."

DIANE: "I understand."

There was a long pause between screen messages. Finally, Diane typed: "Mike? You still there?"

LINTON: "Can I make another request?"

DIANE: "Sure."

LINTON: "About tomorrow?"

DIANE: "Of course."

LINTON: "Wear white stockings."

DIANE: "Excuse me?"

LINTON:	"I still have that Internet image going on in my head."
DIANE:	"I'll see."
LINTON:	"At least wear the earrings."
DIANE:	"Of course. They're beautiful. I wanted to wear them today."
LINTON:	"Not around your husband, please!"
DIANE:	"Anything else?"
LINTON:	"Requests? Am I allowed more?"
DIANE:	"A potential father of my child should be."
LINTON:	"That isn't tomorrow, is it?"
DIANE:	"Nervous?"
LINTON:	"Yes. Very."
DIANE:	"Maybe we can do a dry run."
LINTON:	"What I was hoping for. Yes!"
DIANE:	"I've been thinking about it."
LINTON:	"I can't stop thinking about it."
DIANE:	"I think it would help, don't you?"
LINTON:	"There is a God."
DIANE:	"LOL. It would be good to know we're compatible that way."
LINTON:	"I'm sure we are but a 'dry run' can't hurt. Maybe we should schedule some more."
DIANE:	"LOL. A gross or an even dozen?"
LINTON:	"To familiarize ourselves with each other."
DIANE:	"LOL. You're a man, I'm a woman. It isn't that difficult, Mike."
LINTON:	"You can't fault a man for trying."
DIANE:	"True enough. At least you make the effort."
LINTON:	"So I'll see you tomorrow?"
DIANE:	"I think so. I'll call either way."
LINTON:	"My fingers are crossed."

DIANE:	"Get some sleep."
LINTON:	"One more question."
DIANE:	"Shoot."
LINTON:	"You really wearing a beige thong?"
DIANE:	"Mmmmmmm, yes baby. And it's wet right where you'd think it is. Wait a second while I touch myself. Ahhhhh."
LINTON:	"Enough or I won't make it until tomorrow."
DIANE:	"LOL. Sweet dreams."
Linton:	"Of you. Trust me, of you."

Diane smiled as she logged off and shut down the computer. As she stared at the screen for a long time afterward, however, her smile eventually turned into a frown.

CHAPTER 6

SINGLETON HAD BEEN IN PRISON ONLY SEVEN DAYS when two Dominicans attacked him with metal shanks. He'd managed to disarm one of the attackers, but the other had stabbed him just above his left collarbone and then pulled the shank up his neck to his chin. The wound was deep and rough, leaving the nasty scar.

Federal agents had approached him while he was recovering in a hospital outside of the prison. It was a simple formula, the way that they laid it out for him. He could be a stand-up con and spend the next fifteen years in the joint, or he could be a survivor and get out in two, provided that he was willing to give up the people whom he had worked for. Giving them up hadn't been a difficult decision. Singleton had learned a long time ago that honor among thieves was as real as Santa Claus. All you had to do was read the papers. Even the Italians, with all their ceremony and oaths of honor bullshit, were turning on each other left and right.

Turning was easy for Singleton. Survivors don't question the means to an end.

As he climbed the stairs, Singleton was thinking about relaxing on a Caribbean island. He opened the sweat-stained, blue short-sleeved shirt that he was wearing as he stepped out onto the hot roof of Thomas Jefferson High School in the East New York section of Brooklyn. A heavy man wearing a lot of gold jewelry around his neck and black cyclist shorts with red racing stripes tossed a cigarette over the high wall of the roof.

Singleton dug into his front pants pocket for a pack of cigarettes. He stopped to finger one from the pack and light it.

The heavy man placed a plastic milk crate away from the wall and sat in the shade. Singleton made his way to him without saying a word. The echoing sound of a basketball bouncing against the asphalt school-yard below caught Singleton's attention. He leaned against the high wall and looked down at a two-on-two game directly below. He squinted from the bright sunlight and had to shade his eyes with his right hand.

"You got to get past his mother," the heavy man said. His voice was high-pitched. "She a drunk, so it shouldn't be too hard."

Singleton continued to shield his eyes from the sunlight. "No problem," he said.

The heavy man rubbed his nose and took a long deliberate drag on a fresh Newport cigarette.

Singleton watched the basketball game. A short kid with dyed blonde hair had an awesome jump shot. He sank three consecutive jumpers from the perimeter of the court.

"Damn," Singleton said. "That boy doesn't miss. He playin' for the school here? He should be if he's not."

"Nigga' with the blonde hair?" the heavy man asked.

Singleton nodded.

"He playin' all right," the heavy man said. "But not for no school. For hisself."

Singleton smiled. "For himself or with himself?" he asked.

The heavy man frowned. "What he be is a hustler. Used to run shit for me all the time. When he was nine, ten. Moved up to the bigger shit the last few years. Reggie can't afford to play for this or any other school. Got two different bitches pregnant the same time last year. He a father twice in one week. You see what I'm sayin'? Twice in the same week."

Singleton was still watching the game. The short kid sunk his forth and fifth consecutive jumpers. "I know you do the right thing and all, but that's a goddamn shame," he told the heavy man without looking away from the game. "NBA pay a helluva lot more money than you can, Jamal. Kid with that kind of talent should take his shot before running bullshit on the streets."

The heavy man waved Singleton off. "Man, that one-in-a-billion shit is a pipe dream nobody can afford to chase 'less you seven foot by your thirteenth birthday." He thumbed over his shoulder. "That kid down there barely six foot. Fuckin' midget in the NBA. Just another nigga with a jump shot is all he is."

Singleton turned away from the game. "Ishmael still on Fountain Avenue?" he asked.

The heavy man nodded. "Asleep in his bed," he said. "In a coma." He leaned forward and scratched his right ankle. The gold chains he wore clattered from the movement. "Three fools with three baseball bats, and all they could do was knock him out."

"You send fools, you get fool results," Singleton said.

The heavy man nodded. "Ishmael made some accusations," he said. "Before he got clubbed into that deep sleep."

"I'll bet he did," Singleton said.

"I'm talkin' about some serious shit here," the heavy man said. He tossed the cigarette off the roof and lit a joint. He offered the joint up to Singleton.

Singleton shook off the offer.

"About you and the cops and setting me up for the Dominican thing," the heavy man said. "Ishmael swore it was you gave me up."

Singleton stared hard into the heavy man's eyes. "Ishmael do any fucking time?" he asked. "Ishmael home, ain't he?"

The heavy man returned the stare. "I'm just telling you what Ishmael said."

Singleton maintained eye contact as he took a long drag from his cigarette. "He talk that shit before or after he see the baseball bats?"

The heavy man took another hit off his joint as he broke eye contact.

"You know what it's like inside, Jamal?" Singleton asked. "They shitloads of Dominicans inside. I had to crack one in the head day fucking one to back them down. Day fucking one I was looking at a possible ten-year extension to my own shit." He pointed to his scar. "I got this the next fuckin' week. Day seven in the joint. From two Dominicans slipped through the cracks. It was a push after that. Hundred fifty stitches later, we even, me and the Dominicans. Everything was everything. But they could have killed me just as easy. I was lucky. Some Russians I made a deal with talked the right shit to the right people and saved my ass."

The heavy man nodded. "I heard you got cut," he said. He offered Singleton his joint one more time.

Singleton shook his head again. "Two and a half years, my man," he said. "Two-point-five, and I can go back for picking my fuckin' nose, the law wants to break my balls. I can go back just for being up here on this roof with you right now. Just for associatin'."

"I'm looking at ten minimum," the heavy man said. "Maybe more, Ishmael come out his coma and testify. You see what I'm sayin'? And people do come out, I was told." He snapped his finger for emphasis. "Just like that," he said. "One day they a zombie, the next day they talkin' shit on Jerry fuckin' Springer."

Singleton nodded. "Then I'll take care of it," he said. "I take care of Ishmael and you got nothin' to sweat from me, right? That the point here, ain't it? I need to prove myself with you now. Make my bones like the Italians, right? Like I'm sixteen fuckin' years old, I need to show my stuff one more time. Fine. No problem. I got no problem earnin' my props. I did it before, I do it again." He was showing teeth. "Motherfuck me," he said.

The heavy man smiled. "You all wound up, Jimmy," he said. "The joint made you a nervous mothafucka'."

Singleton shook his finger. "Uh-uh," he said. "Just an angry one. An angry mothafucka', that's what the joint made me."

The heavy man offered Singleton the grass one more time. Singleton tossed his cigarette off the roof and finally accepted it.

* * * * *

Two hours later, Special Agent of the Federal Bureau of Investigation, Eugene Morris, a stocky black man with a thick neck and broad shoulders, followed James Singleton inside an F-train subway car at the West Fourth Street station. He wore a navy blue windbreaker and black sweat pants and carried a small gym bag.

The train was almost empty. Singleton leaned his back against the closed doors as the train jerked into motion. Morris grabbed a handrail and stood in front of Singleton.

"That wasn't so hard," Morris said.

Singleton looked both ways before he glared at Morris. "You jokin', right?"

Morris smiled and looked Singleton up and down. "You're still in one piece," he said.

"That's cute," Singleton said. He took a seat next to a door. "That a reference to the runner they found in Canarsie, right? His legs in one place, the rest of him in the water off the pier there, the crabs snackin' on him like fuckin' chum."

Morris shrugged. "I don't think he felt anything," he said. "There were three bullets in his brain."

"Fuck you," Singleton said.

Morris sat directly across from Singleton. He pulled the sleeve of his windbreaker back to look at his watch and pointed at it.

"You don't have much time," Morris said. "If something don't pan out with the Russians fast, you're probably testifying against Jamal by the end of the month."

"I'm gonna need some room to breathe no matter what I do," Singleton said.

"Room to breathe and fucking off are two different things," Morris said. "We got one report of you and a woman. White woman. That's not what the government had in mind when they made you this deal, Jimmy, slamming the white prize."

Singleton glared at Morris. "I know what I have to do," he said.

Morris leaned back. "Just don't get too comfortable," he said.

The train slowed to a stop at the Fourteenth Street station. Morris bowed his head and closed his eyes when the doors opened. Singleton watched the people leaving and entering the car.

The doors closed, and the train jerked into motion again. Morris opened his eyes, glanced around the car, and leaned forward. "What's up?" he asked Singleton.

"What you think is up?" Singleton said. "I got to prove myself again."

"Meaning?"

Singleton smirked as he stood up. "Trust me," he said. "You don't want to know."

Singleton started to walk toward the far end of the car when Morris called to him.

"Stay in touch!" he yelled.

Singleton raised his right hand up and flipped Morris the bird.

CHAPTER 7

LATE IN THE MORNING, DIANE WOKE EDDIE BY LAYING his buzzing pager on the pillow alongside his head.

"What the hell?" Eddie said, opening his eyes.

"Your pager," Diane said. She was in the process of drying her hair. She sat at the small secretary in their bedroom and switched on the dryer.

Eddie crawled out of bed. He couldn't hear a thing above the noise of the hair dryer. He read his pager display as he walked to the bathroom. He frowned as he recognized the coded telephone number. It was a number he couldn't call from his house.

He called to Diane, "You got coffee started?"

"I didn't have time," she called back.

Eddie went from the bathroom down to the kitchen to make a fresh pot. When he returned to the bedroom, Diane was sitting up in bed smoking. A fashion magazine was opened in her lap.

"So, where were you last night," she asked him. "You never said."

"Business," Eddie said. "It's where I always am when I'm that late."

Diane stubbed out her cigarette. "Right, of course," she said sarcastically. "Business. As in, mind your own."

Eddie rubbed his eyes as he yawned loudly. "Diane, please," he said.

"Please, what?"

"Please don't break them now. It's early. I'm still half in the bag here. I didn't get much sleep."

"Neither did I," Diane said. She lit another cigarette. "Two pairs of white gloves, two pairs of wire cutters, two screwdrivers, two razor-thin box cutters, and two new keys all laid out nice and neat in a shoe box in your closet," she said. "All alongside a new crowbar from The Home Depot. You going into the construction business, Eddie? Or are you and Tommy going shopping again? He called here this morning. So did your agency. They have a legal spot at Clancy this afternoon if you want it. One-on-one with an attorney."

Eddie held up a hand. "Wait a minute," he said. "Tommy called? Why didn't you wake me?"

"I told him you were sleeping," Diane said. "He said he'd call back. He said it wasn't important."

Eddie scratched his head. "What about the job?"

"One-on-one with an attorney at Clancy," Diane said.

"No way," Eddie said.

"I already told the agency," Diane said.

"Jesus Christ!" Eddie said in frustration. "I told them center work only. No one-on-ones. I'm a word-processing center operator. I don't work one-on-ones with fuckin' attorneys who want me to answer their phones, get them coffee, and pick up their lunch. Which agency was it?"

Diane was arranging papers on the secretary. "United?"

"Workers United," Eddie said. "They don't fuckin' listen, you tell them something. None of them hear it. I work in word-processing centers only. They don't fucking listen."

"Anyway," Diane said, "the equipment in the closet?"

Eddie turned away from her. "It's not what you think," he said.

"No, of course it isn't what I'm thinking. You just enrolled in a handyman course, right?"

Eddie was a father by the end of what would have been his senior year of college. He'd taken on a second job and worked hard through his son's third birthday. After watching him struggle working two jobs, Eddie's father had introduced him to the people who would forever change his life.

Although Eddie never romanticized a street life, it had offered a level of independence that was especially appealing at that time in his life. He'd started by running errands for connected guys. He'd learned the importance of "favors" that street guys did for one another and was soon collecting money for bookmakers. He had just started putting his own money on the street, lending it at three points a week, when an incident in a Queens Boulevard nightclub, Bella Bambina, changed him from a knock-around guy to a connected guy.

He was wondering what had happened to that independence when he heard his wife yelling at him again.

"Well?" Diane said. "Did you enroll in a construction course, you and Tommy?"

Eddie frowned. "I didn't say that."

"This is bullshit, Eddie. Whatever you're doing, about to do, it's bullshit."

Eddie glared at her. "Why is it bullshit, Diane?"

"Because of this thing you're going through," she said. "Because I'm doing well and you're not handling it isn't a reason to get yourself put in jail."

Eddie took a deep breath. "I'm glad you're doing well, Diane."

Diane bit her lower lip. "This thing you're going through now. This midlife crisis. It's normal to have one, but you're not handling it. I really wish you would talk to someone."

"A shrink, right?"

"A therapist. A shrink if you need medication, yeah."

"Balls, medication. I need medication, I'll take a fuckin' drink. When I need drugs to make it through the day, do me a favor and put a bullet in my head, put me out of my misery."

"Well, whatever your reason for doing this thing with Tommy now, you know it doesn't make sense. Not when you think it out. We don't need the money, and you don't need to take those kinds of risks anymore. Think of me if you won't think of yourself. It's embarrassing."

Eddie smiled. "You want to fuck your new boss in California so he can get you pregnant, but me going after a score is embarrassing? I guess I'm missing something."

"I wouldn't go anywhere if you would give me a baby," Diane said.

Eddie rolled his eyes. "I can't imagine where this conversation is going," he said.

"Nowhere," Diane said. "Trust me, I gave up on that issue. I gave up last night."

"Please, Diane, I'm dog-tired. I got things to do today. I don't have time for this now."

"Right, Eddie, of course you don't."

Eddie clenched his teeth. "I fucking hate when you say that, 'Right, Eddie, of course you don't'."

Diane ignored his mocking voice. "You're avoiding the problem. You're not dealing with your problem."

"Because I don't want to pay some con-artist to listen to what you say is my problem? Because I don't want to pop Valium instead of answer the telephone? Please."

"Fine," she said, frustrated. "Forget therapy. Forget that for now. You can't deny that we don't need the money from what you and Tommy are planning. You can't deny that whatever it is you're planning is too risky. You don't need to take those risks anymore."

"Don't tell me what I don't need, Diane," Eddie said as he lit a cigarette. "I have boring fucking computer skills and some street money coming in. Not near what I used to have coming in off the street, by the way, and no new irons in the fire. I got the same old shit, day to day, Diane. You said the agency called, right? That's what it is. I'm supposed to get excited waiting on word-processing calls? Please. I'm not defending what the fuck I'm doing with Tommy now, but I'm sure as shit not explaining myself to you about it, either."

On the advice of the man who had brought him along, Eddie had learned a skill that would keep him from being sucked into a street life.

"Learn how to do X rays or somethin'," Joe Sharpetti had told him. "Or computers or some shit. Anything that'll draw attention away from what you do with me is good. All these other guys, as hard as they are, they got nothin' else. The government wants them, the police, it isn't hard to know where to look. They got no jobs, and they wear a Rolex. They pay no income tax, but they drive a fuckin' Lexus. You see what I'm saying? Teach yourself something you can fall back on. Like your mother used to tell you, you need somethin' to fall back on. This life I live, these other guys want so bad, it ain't a long life. You're ever in doubt about that, read the fuckin' papers."

Eddie had followed Sharpetti's advice and taught himself how to type with a software program he had purchased with a new computer. One year to the day that he had bought the computer, Eddie was hired by a major financial institution in New York as a graveyard shift word-processing operator. Six months later, he quit his window-cleaning job and was working the street by day and a computer by night.

The life that he led was profitable but lonely. When he first met her, Diane was a challenge for Eddie. She was aggressive. She was smart. She was sexy. She was a challenge.

Now, since she had awakened him this morning, Diane was a pain in the ass.

"I'm your wife, damn it!" she yelled.

"You sure? Maybe you have me confused with somebody on AOL."

Diane slammed her hairbrush down on the secretary. "Damn it, Eddie."

Eddie remained calm. "I'm not explaining myself," he repeated.

"Because you can't have someone to answer to," Diane said. She crushed out her cigarette.

"If you mean you, yeah, you're right," Eddie said. "I won't answer to you."

Diane lit another cigarette. "Why not? Why won't you answer to me?"

"Please."

"That's not an answer, Eddie."

"It'll have to do."

"Another cop-out."

Eddie scratched his chin. "What is so hard for you to understand here? I'm not the type of guy to explain myself, Diane. It's half the reason I do what I do. So I don't have to explain myself. So I don't have to answer to people."

"So you don't have to deal with people," Diane said.

Eddie rubbed his forehead. "Right," he said. "Exactly."

"Yeah, well, that's a great way to go through life, Eddie. Is that what you tell Jack? If you don't like somebody, make sure you have a way of telling them to go fuck themselves?"

"It isn't bad my kid grows up with a pair of balls," Eddie said.

"Bullshit," Diane said. "Do you really want Jack to go through life with a chip on his shoulder because he can't take criticism? Because he doesn't like to be told something? Because he's afraid of something new? I don't think so."

Eddie took a few deep breaths. "Look," he said. "Nothing is going to happen. Everything will be all right."

"You've been lucky so far," Diane said. "Everybody is lucky for a while. And then their luck changes, and they get fucked. Only it's not only you who gets fucked anymore. You should have some consideration for me, too." Diane put her hands on her hips. "You were lucky for a long time, Eddie," she said. "All those assholes you deal with. How many times has it been you had to bail out Tommy with Joe Sharp? How many times did he get himself in trouble betting sports? And every one of those guys would sell you down the river in a heartbeat. Tommy included, and you know it."

"If I promise this is the last time, would you believe me?" he asked.

"No," Diane said.

Eddie crushed out his cigarette. "When are you going to California?" he asked.

"I don't know," Diane said.

"You sure about this thing with your new boss?"

"No," Diane said, sniffling. "I'm not sure about anything right now."

Eddie took another deep breath. "At least now you're making some sense," he said.

They were both uncomfortable. Eddie finally broke the silence. "Look, let's try and be civil a couple days until things get sorted out, all right? If you still want to go through with this guy, then fine. We'll do whatever we have to do. Let's just be civil in the meantime, all right? Let's not break each other's balls."

Diane frowned at her husband.

"What?" Eddie asked.

"You have a way with words, Eddie," Diane said. "You have such a way with words."

CHAPTER 8

THEY WERE TEN YEARS OLD. THEY HAD COME HOME from playing stickball at the grammar school. Tommy had hit a home run to win the game and was excited. A police car was parked in front of his house. Two officers were at the door talking to his mother. Eddie and Tommy stopped at the front gate, unsure of what was going on. When Tommy's mother let out a long loud wail, both boys were startled.

A few minutes later, Eddie learned what had happened. He remembered being shocked and having to step back from the look on his friend's face when Tommy learned that his father had died from a sudden heart attack. Eddie remembered choking on his own emotions. He remembered feeling tears on his cheeks before it seemed like Tommy could even breathe again.

He had felt obligated to look after his friend ever since. He would do so several times throughout their lives. He was doing it again now.

"I didn't want to say anything about this," Tommy said.

"It's none of my business," Eddie said.

They were standing outside of the trailer office of a used-car lot on

Queens Boulevard. A light drizzle started. Tommy moved to one side to make room for Eddie to stand under the awning.

"How much you owe this guy?" Eddie asked.

"Fifteen-five," Tommy said. He pulled at one end of his mustache. "For going on three weeks now. I think I'm the only guy in New York bet the Yankees three straight nights and lost."

Eddie smiled. "What were you laying?"

Tommy waived him off. "You don't wanna know," he said. "I got crippled starting with a simple twenty time bet. You know how it goes. One hundred turns into two, turns into . . . ."

"Fifteen-five," Eddie said. "You're right, I don't want to know."

The door to the trailer office opened. A tall man with a thick gold bracelet waved them inside. Eddie let Tommy in ahead of him. He eyeballed the tall man as he stepped inside of the trailer.

"Who's this?" a fat man sitting behind a desk asked Tommy, pointing at Eddie.

"A friend of mine," Tommy said. "Eddie Senta."

Eddie extended a hand but the fat man ignored him.

"He here to pay off your debt?" the fat man asked.

Tommy shook his head as he scratched at his mustache.

"He your meat?" the fat man asked. "He's a big guy, I'm supposed to get nervous? That it?"

Tommy shook his head again.

The fat man held out a hand. "Where's my money?" he asked Tommy.

Eddie pulled out his wallet. He pulled five hundred-dollar bills from the wallet and dropped them on the desk. "Take that for now," he said.

"Excuse me?" the fat man said. He ignored the bills.

Eddie frowned at Tommy.

"Excuse me?" the fat man repeated.

Eddie glared into the fat man's eyes. "Take that for now," he said.

"He doesn't have the rest right now. He will by the end of the week. I guarantee it."

"Really?" the fat man asked sarcastically.

"Really," Eddie said.

"Maybe I don't want it next week," the fat man said. "Since I been waitin' on this fuckin' money for more than three weeks already. Maybe I don't give a fuck you throw down a few hundred dollars to buy him some time."

Eddie was still glaring into the fat man's eyes. "You the one called his house, yelled at his wife?"

The fat man moved up on his chair. "The fuck business is it of yours?" he asked.

"You're lucky he's giving you anything," Eddie said. "Scaring a woman like that. That must have took balls, huh?"

The tall man stepped up alongside Eddie. "I'm the one made the call," he said.

Eddie turned to face the tall man. "Then you're a jerk-off," he said.

The tall man's face twitched. Eddie showed teeth as he glared at the tall man.

"If you came here to look for trouble," the fat man said, "if that's what you want for your friend here, I hope you realize what you're dealing with."

Eddie turned toward the fat man again. "You hope I got a wise-guy friend, you mean," he said. "A somebody to talk to your somebody. Because I already called your tough-guy bluff and that's the only thing you have left now is some wiseguy."

"Who the fuck is this guy?" the tall man asked Tommy.

"Who's your friend?" the fat man asked Eddie.

"That's my business," Eddie said. "And I'm not interested in who your wise-guy friend is. This is a simple situation. The man lost money to your book. He went in over his head. He's not the first, and he won't be the last. He's here now, by your request, after your numbskull scared the shit out of his wife, and he drops five hundred on your desk. So, you take the five and he owes you ten-five. He'll have that next week. If that's not good enough, if you feel you need to get your rocks off playing a role, you can go and fuck yourself. You and the telephone tough guy likes to terrorize women."

The fat man counted the money on his desk. He looked up at Eddie, thought about saying something else, and then waved him away.

"Right," Eddie said.

"See you next week," Tommy said.

* * * * *

"That took balls," Tommy said to Eddie as they were getting into the Lincoln Town Car.

"So was laying three-to-one on a slumping Yankee team three nights in a row," Eddie said.

Tommy pointed a finger at Eddie as he started the car. "That was stupid," he said.

"I need you to drop me in the city," Eddie said.

"Sure," Tommy said. "After what you just did, name your state."

Eddie lit a cigarette. Tommy looked at Eddie as he drove.

"You pissed?" Tommy asked.

Eddie was preoccupied. "Huh?"

"You angry at me?" Tommy asked again. "I don't blame you, you are. I know Joe Sharp had his fill reaching out for me. I wouldn't ask you to do that again."

Eddie shook his head. "I saw something last night after I dropped you off," he said. "On my way home. I circled back where the office is. I saw something bothered me."

Tommy was curious. "Cops?" he asked.

Eddie shook his head again. "A third party," he said.

"Huh?" Tommy said.

Eddie waved it off. "Forget about it," he said. "Probably nothing. I'm headed there again now to check on things. Can you be ready in a couple days if we have to go?"

"This is the car," Tommy said. "I had one of my customers drop it off, until further notice. Guy's backed up on me two weeks."

"Remind me and I'll split it with you, the cost," Eddie said. "For however long you keep the car."

Tommy spoke in an exaggerated street voice. "I'm ready tonight, we have to go, Eddie. Ab-so-tute-ly, positively."

Eddie smiled. "Who was that, O.J.?" he asked. "The ab-so-tute-ly."

Tommy shook his head. "IMUS doing O.J." he said.

Eddie laughed. "The I-Man," he said.

"Hey, last time when these guys tonight called and I answered the phone, I did my Jerry Seinfeld," Tommy said. "You should've heard that conversation. The tall dick, I guess it was, screamin' at me over the phone and me doing Jerry Seinfeld back at him." Tommy went into an exaggerated whiny Jerry Seinfeld voice. "Sorry, sir, Tommy isn't home right now. I don't know where he is. How should I know where he is? Am I Tommy's keeper?"

Eddie was shaking his head as he laughed. "You got a clear fucking head," he said. "Jerry Seinfeld. Jesus Christ."

"You working tonight?" Tommy asked. "The computers?"

"No," Eddie said. "Not tonight. Why?"

"Maybe we go get a drink," Tommy said. "To celebrate."

Eddie made a face. "Celebrate what?"

"I don't know," Tommy said. "Jerry Seinfeld. Who gives a fuck."

Eddie started to laugh hard. His face turned red as his body jerked from spasms of laughter.

"Hey, it wasn't that funny," Tommy said.

Eddie couldn't speak. His eyes started to tear from laughing.

"Hey!" Tommy said again.

Eddie couldn't control himself. He spoke through his laughter. "Jerry Seinfeld," he said.

Tommy started to laugh himself. "Hey!" he said through the laughter. "We're a pair of fucking clowns."

Eddie slapped at the dashboard. Both men continued to laugh hysterically as Tommy drove the length of Queens Boulevard.

* * * * *

Ten hours after flipping the federal agent the bird, James Singleton had a taxi cab drop him off on Flatlands and Louisiana Avenues in Brooklyn. It was just after one o'clock in the morning. Louisiana Avenue was quiet except for a stray dog pawing at strewn garbage. Singleton walked about two miles to an address on Fountain Avenue. He used the back entrance of a twelve-story apartment building and then walked up a dark stairwell three flights.

Singleton checked the hallway several times before leaving the safety of the stairwell to find apartment 3-E. He tried the doorknob, but it was locked, so he used a penknife to pick the lock. He worked fast and was soon inside the nearly dark two-bedroom apartment.

A light was on in the living room to the right of the doorway. Singleton looked inside the room, seeing that the television was on. An older black woman was snoring lightly in an armchair directly in front of the television. Several empty beer cans littered the snack tray to the right of the armchair.

Singleton removed his sneakers and took careful steps to the opposite end of the apartment, where both bedrooms and the bathroom were located. The smaller of the bedrooms was the last room on the left. The door to the room was wide open. Singleton saw his former partner, Ismael Hawkins, sleeping in the propped-up hospital bed. An intravenous drip bag hung from a stand on one side of the bed.

Singleton noticed a foul odor as soon as he was inside the room. He spotted the bedpan at the foot of the bed and shook his head at the sight. He closed the bedroom door behind him and leaned against a portable table with an extended tray. He used the table to balance himself while he slipped his sneakers on. He jerked his hand off the table when a cockroach ran across his fingers.

Singleton stepped close to the side of the bed to look for signs of life. Ishmael was breathing, but the movement of his chest was slight. The twenty-eight-year-old's eyes were open, but they appeared to be fixed on a spot high on the far wall.

He had seen that same stare in prison. Once a man was broken down, his eyes would reflect his defeat. The animal instincts of the population would take over, and the broken man would become instant prey. That dead stare was part of an unconscious body language that marked victims without their ever knowing it.

Singleton frowned at his former partner. "I doin' you a big favor," he whispered.

Singleton covered the .380 with a pillow that he pulled from under Hawkins' head. He pressed the pillow against the comatose man's left ear and squeezed off two quick shots. Ishmael's head jerked to the right in death. The noise from the shots was minimal. Singleton jammed the gun inside of his pants and pushed himself away from the bed. He leaned against the bedroom door to listen for Hawkins' mother, but silence quickly refilled the room.

Singleton carefully let himself out of the apartment. He walked back down the three flights of stairs and was out of the building within three minutes of killing his former partner. He started to retrace his path back to Louisiana Avenue when he spotted a Toyota Camry without a steering wheel lock parked on the street.

CHAPTER 9

ARLY IN THE MORNING, SARAH PARKER WAS CALLED into Larry Singotti's office. He was sitting in the red leather armchair across from the brown couch. He was a short, thin man with black dye in his hair that made him appear younger than his fifty-six years.

Singotti was busy lighting his pipe when Sarah entered his office. She waited until he lit the pipe, took a few drags, and set the pipe down in an ashtray.

"What's up?" Sarah asked from the doorway. Her eyes were tired. She rubbed them with both fists as she yawned.

Singotti pointed behind Sarah. "Close the door," he said.

Sarah closed the door and took a seat on the brown couch. She was wearing a red leather skirt and a tight black pullover top. Singotti eyed her legs as Sarah crossed them on the couch. He shifted his focus from her legs to her breasts.

"You remember Ivan Greenbaum?" he asked. He reached for his cup of coffee. "My friend from the Caribbean? I think you met him here once before. Short, fat, stringy gray hair. He's a jeweler."

"Sure," Sarah said. "The guy who always looks dirty and, if you get close enough, smells dirty."

Singotti smiled. "Yes, that's him."

Sarah moved up on the couch. "Can I grab a cup first?" she asked.

Singotti held up a hand. "This will only take a minute."

Sarah sat back on the couch. "I took some messages from him the last few days. Is he still coming? You need me to arrange a car?"

"Huh?" Singotti said.

"Your friend. Do you need me to arrange a car for him again? I did that the last time. Ring-a-Car picked him up at Kennedy."

"Oh, no, not that," Singotti said. He sipped his coffee, wiping his mouth with a napkin and setting down the cup. "Actually," he said, "I need your help with something else."

Sarah was eyeing Singotti's coffee. "I could really use a cup of coffee, Larry," she said.

He lit his pipe again, took a few deliberate puffs from it, and signaled Sarah to go get her coffee. He watched her ass as she left his office. He set the pipe back down in the ashtray when she reappeared with her cup of coffee in hand.

"Thanks," she said. "I really needed this." She sipped the coffee several times before looking at Singotti again.

"Okay?" he asked, after Sarah had finished her first few sips.

"Sorry," she said.

"Actually," Singotti continued, "I was wondering how your sex life has been."

Sarah made a face. "Excuse me?"

Singotti smirked. "Well, you know. Have you been getting any lately? I know we haven't been together in a while. It's been, what, three or four months, right?"

"Almost six," Sarah said without emotion.

"Six," Singotti said. "I knew it was a while."

"If you count blow jobs," Sarah said. "It's been since that incident in the office with that temp that you even touched me."

"Yes, well," Singotti said.

"I figured he scared you off," Sarah said. "It could just as easily have been your wife."

Singotti fidgeted. "Well," he continued, "how is it? Your sex life."

Sarah paused a moment. "Ah, stalled," she said, still without emotion.

"So you're not getting any?" Singotti asked.

Sarah looked up at the ceiling before answering. "What is it you want help with, Larry?"

Singotti held a smile.

"Well?" she asked again.

Singotti shrugged. "I was just wondering," he said. "Whether or not you were involved with anyone or, if you'd like to meet somebody."

"The dirty guy?" Sarah asked, shocked at the thought.

"Well, he's not that bad," Singotti said. "Not once you clean him up. Make him take a shower and so on."

"I don't believe this," Sarah said.

"He's a very dear friend," Singotti said. "And I can guarantee he's nothing like . . . well, you know."

Sarah rolled her eyes. Singotti talked through his discomfort. "Hell, you already know Ivan," he said. "He's like a lamb. A fat, roly-poly, little lamb. He couldn't hurt a fly if he wanted to."

Sarah took a deep breath. "A roly-poly, little lamb who doesn't bathe," she said.

Singotti shot her a frown. "He's a friend, Sarah."

"As in?"

"He's a friend. He does me favors. I like to do him favors back. We do business together."

"Like me? In other words, favors like me. You want to pimp me off. For what? I hope it's something valuable."

Singotti grabbed for his pipe again. "I didn't think you'd react this way," he said. "I didn't think it was this big a deal. The man is fucking harmless. You could probably get him off in twenty seconds and be on your way. And you'd make my life and your life a lot easier, wouldn't you?"

"So I'd better come to my senses, I'm sure," Sarah said.

Singotti glared at her as he relit the pipe. "I didn't say that. That is up to you, Sarah. I'm not forcing you to do anything. I've never forced you."

Sarah smirked. "Right," she said. "Let's not kid ourselves here, Larry. I can live with it a lot easier if it's clear between us. I can't afford to be so charitable anymore. I'm getting older by the day, just like everybody else in the world."

Singotti set down his pipe. "Are you asking me for money?" he asked.

Sarah sat forward on the couch. "Are you asking me to fuck your friend?"

Singotti smiled. "Touché," he said.

CHAPTER 10

I WAS HOPING YOU WEREN'T DRINKING AGAIN," EDDIE told Sarah.

She'd been drinking ginger ale when Eddie arrived at her apartment early that afternoon. She drained her glass. "It's been a long morning," she said. "And I'm not drinking again. Not yet."

Eddie placed his jacket over the back of a worn black leather couch directly across from the equally worn green cloth recliner in which Sarah sat. He lit a cigarette and moved an ashtray closer to his reach.

"I was in the neighborhood the other night," Eddie said. "Driving a friend around, looking the area over."

"Casing the place," Sarah said. "I get it."

"Right," Eddie said. "And after I drop him off where he parked his car, I decide to take the Triborough Bridge back to the Grand Central out to the Island."

"It's a lovely bridge," Sarah said.

"Yeah, it is," Eddie said. "So I decided I'd take Third Avenue uptown to get to the bridge, you know, instead of the Drive. I take Third Avenue up around here for one more pass, and who do I see coming out of that bar, Name The Joint, or whatever it is. I see you and some black dude has one of his hands pasted to your ass. The both of you walking a little cockeyed, if you know what I mean."

Sarah smiled. "Are you jealous, Eddie?"

"Maybe. What's the difference, if you're drinking again?"

"I'm not, I told you. That was James. He was drinking. I was an observer."

Eddie took a long drag on his cigarette. "That's good company for a drunk to keep," he said. "Another drunk."

"He's a convict," Sarah said. "Tell you the truth."

"Oh, great," Eddie said. He crushed out his cigarette. "That's just what I needed to hear."

Sarah held up both her hands. "He doesn't know anything," she said. "He's just somebody I met a few days ago. I didn't think I had to clear that sort of thing with you."

Eddie squinted at Sarah. "A drunken con?" he said. "I'll bet your sponsor in the program thinks that's a great idea."

"We're friends, Eddie," Sarah said. "We're not getting married or anything. And I would never jeopardize anything that you're involved in. You should know me better than that. I appreciate all you've done for me. All you keep doing. James is just somebody I met, and I'm not so stupid as to tell a guy who did time for robbery about a fifteen-thousand-dollar job. Nor am I so gullible as to think he's in love with me. I know my own history with men. It sucks. And I'm sure he's just another notch in my belt of abusive men. Only he hasn't started any of that yet, so right now it's just lust and some company. Or some company and lust. Nothing more, nothing less."

Eddie had been staring into Sarah's eyes while she'd been speaking. He lit another cigarette. "Robbery?" he said. "That's pretty general."

"He said nobody was hurt," Sarah said.

"I'm not saying you shouldn't have a private life," Eddie said. "I'm just saying you should be more careful about who it's with."

"Well, he's articulate," Sarah said. "If that makes a difference."

"Most con men are," Eddie said.

Sarah was shaking her head. "He's got an education. Or he's self-taught. He's not just another street bum, Eddie. He isn't so bad when he isn't laying it on thick, the street talk. He thinks I expect it from him. But he slips every now and then, and I know he's playing a role with the street talk."

"Maybe the role he's playing is the articulate one," Eddie said. "A good con artist can cover a lot of ground, Sarah. If he's polished, it's not exactly the same thing as being educated."

Sarah sat up in her chair. "Because if he was educated, he wouldn't be a convict, right?"

"Something like that."

"And what about you? You're educated, and you're a criminal."

Eddie laughed. "Criminal and convict are two different things, kid."

"Yeah, one of you was caught."

"Yeah, well, I'm only a criminal sometimes, Sarah," Eddie continued. "And always by choice. There's a difference."

Now Sarah laughed. "Right," she said. "Of course. What made me think your crimes aren't crimes of choice?"

For a brief period after she had taken him to lunch, Sarah had thought that she and Eddie might have something together. He was attentive and concerned, and he tried to get her off the drink. He had also offered to help her find a new job.

It was after she'd declined his help and Eddie had continued to be there for her that Sarah realized that what they had was a special friendship. Eddie was a decent guy. He cared about people other than himself. He cared about her.

When Singotti's colleague had raped and assaulted her, and later was hospitalized with broken legs, Sarah knew that Eddie was more complicated than she had first thought. There was a dark side to his personality that most people never saw. It was intense and dangerous. It seemed to lurk just beneath the decent guy.

Eddie waved her off. "Anyway, I am concerned about your articulate alcoholic convict friend knowing something about this score. Pillow talk can go a long way to fuck up a wet dream."

Sarah crushed out her cigarette. "James doesn't know a thing about this," she said. "I'm not looking to get him back into trouble, nor am I looking to get you or myself into trouble. Actually, to tell you the truth, he's somebody I met in a bar a few nights ago who stopped me from taking a drink. And he's managed to do that ever since. I promise you, Eddie, he doesn't know a thing."

"I hope not," Eddie said. "Because my friend likes the way this looks and so do I, minus James the articulate convict."

Sarah smiled. "So you're over your fear of making a move this late in life?"

"Well, I really don't need to do this right now," Eddie said, sitting back on the couch. "I don't really need the cash or the risk."

"That was the story the last few times we talked," Sarah said. "Although I have to tell you, I think it's just your way. To discuss the risks with yourself out loud, to hear yourself say it, then do what you really want to do anyway."

"It's a tough thing to turn away from, five grand in cash," Eddie said. "Especially when you can keep it on the side, nobody knows about it."

"On the side like me?" Sarah said. "To look at but not touch?"

"I'm serious," Eddie said. "Because you never know, right? Things don't work out the way you count, the boiler breaks, the roof gets a hole in it, the pipes burst . . . ."

"Your wife slaps you with a divorce," Sarah added.

"That, too, yeah. In fact, I think that's more likely than not. Or that I slap her with one."

Sarah reached for her cigarettes. "This the part where you cry the blues about you and your wife and how you feel like this is really it this time? You're getting a divorce because she wants a kid and you don't, and she's making all kinds of legitimate money, and you're still just a street guy, and it's what the celebrities call 'irreconcilable differences'?"

"You rehearse that?" Eddie asked.

"Let me tell you something, Eddie," Sarah said. She stopped to light her cigarette. "You're a street-smart guy but sometimes even street-smart guys can't see the forest for the trees. For all you know, she has one foot out the door already. For all you know, she's the one with somebody on the side and you keep passing on the truly loyal women of the world like myself."

Eddie smiled. "Yeah, well, I think about that, too, sometimes," he said.

Sarah poured herself another ginger ale. Eddie reached across the table for the glass, lifting it to smell the soda.

"Please don't tell me you're going to give this woman a baby, Eddie," Sarah said. "Please don't tell me that."

"Of course I'm not," Eddie said. "Not while I got one kid I fucked up with already. I don't need another one I can't put to bed because I live in another county."

"I wouldn't beat myself up over that."

"It's true. I'm not exactly father of the year here."

Sarah took a long drag on her cigarette. "Nor are you the only divorced father in the world," she said. "You should read the statistics sometime. It happens ten thousand times an hour. Parents get divorced all the time."

"Yeah, well, it doesn't lessen the guilt," Eddie said. "Knowing the statistics. Knowing you're one of them."

"I'm just saying you shouldn't beat yourself up over your son," Sarah said. "You do the right thing by him."

Eddie shook his head. "I'm a good provider," he said. "I'm not a good father. There's a difference."

"Well, there's a lot to be said for being a good provider," Sarah said. "There are deadbeat dads out there don't even do that much."

"You're comparing me to deadbeats," Eddie said. "That isn't exactly a compliment."

"You know what I mean," Sarah said. "I think sometimes you wallow in this guilt shit about your kid."

Eddie waved her off again. "What do you know?"

Sarah counted off on her fingers. "Enough not to have kids," she said. "Enough not to get married. Enough not to take your melodramatic parental concerns very serious."

Eddie sat back on the couch. "Oh, really? And why is that?"

"Because, essentially, Eddie, my dear, you're here to discuss robbing an office," Sarah said. "Behind all this concern for your kid and your shitty marriage, you're talking about grand larceny."

Eddie's eyebrows furrowed. "This is you talking here, right? The same one who's feeding me this score, right? The one brought the idea to me, no? Maybe you're the one confused."

"Yes, and I'm not the one crying about tucking my kid in, either," Sarah said. "I know exactly what I'm doing. For me, it's revenge more than money. For me, it's a chance to strike back through you, Eddie. Call me a coward, but don't call me confused."

Eddie glanced at his watch. "This has been great, this psychoanalysis, Sarah, but I have to get back to Brooklyn and try to see Jack tonight."

Sarah took another long drag on her cigarette.

"He withdrew fifteen thousand dollars yesterday?" Eddie asked.

Sarah nodded. "From a safe deposit box. I saw the envelope in his desk drawer. It was marked. '15K'."

"And the guy is bringing the gold tonight, right? You're not sure when they're meeting but probably this weekend, right? Saturday or maybe Sunday."

"Unless they meet tonight," Sarah said. "Which I doubt because I had to arrange a lunch reservation for Larry this afternoon and I know he's going to the theatre with his wife tonight."

"And the cleaning crew doesn't work until Monday night."

"They're off weekends, Saturdays and Sundays."

"So the place is empty until Monday morning?"

"Theoretically, yes."

"Theoretically. And if there's nothing there, I can take the computers?"

"You'd be crazy not to. All that trouble otherwise for nothing."

"Fifteen grand is a lot of scratch for one night's work," Eddie said.

"Need it or not," Sarah said, "it certainly is. Now, I have to get back to the office before I lose track of what's going on."

Eddie sucked hard on his cigarette. "You really off the sauce?"

"Yes," Sarah said. She crossed herself. "Swear to God, and hope to die."

"Good girl," Eddie said.

CHAPTER 11

SHORTLY AFTER EDDIE LEFT SARAH'S APARTMENT, Singleton arrived carrying a box with a black kitten inside. Sarah was about to leave to get back to work. She was startled by Singleton.

"What's that?" she asked, staring at the box.

Singleton smiled. The kitten cried from inside the box. Singleton winked as he held the box up to Sarah.

"Oh, my God!" Sarah said. She reached into the box and picked up the kitten. She kissed its head and held it against her chest. "It's so cute."

Singleton set the box on the living room floor. A bag of cat food, a towel, and a string toy also were inside of the box. "Well, it's not like having a baby," he said, "but the man sold it to me said it takes a commitment, owning a pet."

Tears welled as she kissed the kitten. "It does," she said. "It's why I never bought one for myself while I was drinking."

Singleton grabbed a small bowl from a kitchen cabinet and poured in some of the cat food, setting the bowl on the floor. "I actually wondered about that," he said. "Why you don't have a pet, living alone and all. I wondered if it was the booze."

Sarah nodded. "Because of the drinking," she said. She nestled her nose in the kitten's fur. "Yes, yes, yes," she said.

Singleton took the kitten from Sarah and put it on the floor next to the bowl. The kitten immediately started to eat. "Well, you stopped the drinking," he said. "I seen that for myself. So, now you have a cat to take care of. It's a girl cat, so it has to go back and get the knife. Man said that's part of the deal, from where I got it."

"What should I name it?" Sarah asked as she kneeled down to pet the kitten.

"I guess pussy is too crude, huh?" Singleton asked.

"Yes, it is," Sarah said with a frown. "I want to give it a nice name. A pretty name."

"How 'bout Yolanda?" Singleton asked.

Sarah made a face. "Who's that?"

"My mom's," Singleton said.

"Your mother? Really?" Sarah asked. Singleton nodded. Sarah closed one eye and thought about it. "Okay," she said, after a while. "Yolanda she is. Yes, yes, yes. Yolanda is your name, pretty girl."

* * * * *

Ten minutes later, while Sarah was combing her hair in the bathroom, Singleton spotted her personal telephone book on the kitchen counter. He looked through it until he found Eddie Senta's name. He wrote his address and telephone numbers on a scrap of paper. When he was finished, he picked up the kitten and carried it into the living room.

"I saw the man was here," Singleton said as he sat down in the armchair. "Big shoulders, curly hair. Italian-lookin' dude. Drives a Saab, right? I was just about to come up. Me and Yolanda here had to wait down the street until he was gone."

"He came to check on things," Sarah said. "He saw us together the other night. He was nervous about you knowing what was going on."

"The way I'm nervous about him knowing what's up?"

"I guess."

"There's nobody else in this neither of us know about, I hope," Singleton said. "I hope you not playing both sides against the middle, baby. That wouldn't be right. Not to your friend or to me."

Sarah stopped combing her hair. She stood in the bathroom doorway. "Of course not," she said. "This started with Eddie and then I met you. I probably never should have mentioned this to you."

Singleton searched for the television remote from the armchair. "You know I'm hurting for money is why you mentioned it," he said. "Seeing you got an inside track and all. You know it's not a dangerous thing we about to do."

"I'm not so sure anymore," Sarah said as she combed her hair again. "The closer it gets, the more nervous I am."

"That's natural," Singleton said. "This not your type of thing. Plus you're a woman. That makes it twice as hard."

Sarah stopped combing her hair. "I'm just scared," she said. "I don't want anything to go wrong. I once stole a pair of shorts from a clothing store when I was a teenager, and I was sick over it for days. I wouldn't go out of my house, and I never even wore the damn things."

Singleton was smiling. "I think I like that story," he said. "Tells me something about you. You not the type to work me and your friend against each other."

Sarah rolled her eyes. "Are you kidding me?" she said. "Tell me you're not serious about that."

"Man's got to be careful, baby," Singleton said. He looked down at the kitten. "Right, Yolanda? 'Specially a man just come out. Can't afford no sucker punches might land me on my black ass back upstate. Prison be an ugly place, baby. Real ugly."

"I would never do something like that," Sarah said. "And I feel terrible lying to Eddie about you. At least you know he's going after the cash. He doesn't even know we're going after the gold. He doesn't have a clue."

"You could just back him off," Singleton said. "Just leave the cash to us, me and you, and we can forget the gold. That be just as simple. Then you don't have to worry about your friend anymore."

Sarah frowned as she went into the bathroom to check her appearance. "I don't want to disappoint him," she said. "He was involved before you. He went through a lot of trouble to arrange what he's doing. I can't just cut him out. I owe him. I told you about that. I owe Eddie a lot."

"You could lie, baby," Singleton said. "You can call him, tell him it's off. The man with the gold changed his mind, got a better price somewhere else. The man with the money is getting an unexpected divorce, needs to hang on to every dime. You can make something up."

Sarah frowned at herself in the bathroom mirror. "I can't do that," she said. "If he ever found out, I could never face him again. He's a real friend, Jimmy. I won't do that to Eddie."

Singleton raised both his hands. "Cool," he said. "That's cool with me. I was just making a suggestion, baby. To ease some of this concern of yours, that's all. It just be a lot easier, we do this thing with the cash ourselves. Then you still want to cut him in, you could do that, too. Give him some money for his past efforts and all."

"Then he'd know I did it without him," Sarah said. "I can't do that."

"I guess," Singleton said. He scratched at the kitten's neck. The kitten yawned as it started to stretch. Its nails dug into Singleton's chest. He nearly jumped out of his chair as the kitten jumped off him. "Damn!" he yelled. "Mother fuck me!"

Sarah ran out of the bathroom when she heard Singleton yell.

"What happened?" She saw Singleton checking his chest for blood. She picked up the kitten and cuddled it against her shoulder.

"Yolanda clawed me," Singleton said. He was still feeling under his shirt for blood. "God damn, that hurt."

"She needs a scratch post," Sarah said. "I'll pick one up on the way home."

Singleton was still checking himself for blood. "I hope you do," he said.

"I will," Sarah said. "Maybe you better let her lay on the bed and sleep some. She doesn't know she hurt you."

"I hope not," Singleton said, "or we gonna have a problem, me and Yolanda."

Sarah kissed the kitten on the head. She brought it into the bedroom, closing the door behind her when she came out.

"I have to get back to work," she said. "I'll call you later. If the phone rings, don't forget to let the machine pick up. It might be Eddie."

"Right," Singleton said.

Sarah kissed Singleton hard on the mouth. "And I love Yolanda," she said. "Thank you."

Singleton squeezed Sarah's ass. "You can thank me later, baby."

Sarah grabbed at Singleton's crotch. "I will," she said. "I promise."

CHAPTER 12

DIANE WAS A LATE-BLOOMER. SHE HAD REJECTED THE strict discipline of her parents while growing up in their Long Island home. She rebelled against their expectations and her Jewish faith. She attained average grades and attended a community college instead of the private universities that her parents had wished for.

She had married a man eight years her senior before she finished her degree. Although she had never gotten pregnant during her marriage, it was not from lack of trying. Her husband had been sterile.

In her early thirties, aging had blessed Diane. Her once-thin build was suddenly sexy. Men were attentive, and women were envious. Her makeover from a rebellious daughter to a successful woman was complete, except for getting a new man.

By the time that Eddie Senta came along, Diane was ready to explode into worlds she had only imagined before. At first, life with Eddie was fast and exciting. He knew things that she could never imagine knowing. He interacted with dangerous people and took risks that other people only dreamed of. He was a natural in an adventurous and exhilarating environment.

As Diane succeeded in business, however, the excitement of her husband's world faded quickly. And at a point in her life when she was financially secure, Diane decided that she wanted a child.

It was time to restructure her life one more time. Eddie might or might not be a part of the new life. Whether he would be was a question that she had been asking herself over and over lately. It was the question that she would ignore today.

She was nervous as she entered the Plaza Hotel lobby. She struggled to finger a cigarette from her purse. She was dressed in a white skirt suit with brown high heels, white nylons, and her favorite pearls. She was also wearing an expensive pair of diamond stud earrings that her husband knew nothing about.

When she was more composed, Diane used one of the lobby telephones to call the man she was there to see. Mike Linton answered on the second ring.

"I'm downstairs," Diane said nervously. She was looking at her hands. "My hands are shaking."

"I'll come right down," Linton said.

"No," Diane said. "I'll just come up. I'm too nervous. I'm fucking terrified. I think I need a drink."

"I'll order," Linton said.

"Right," Diane said.

* * * * *

Fifteen minutes later, she was sipping white wine as she stood at the window of Linton's two-room suite, staring down at the carriages on the edge of Central Park. The day had turned gray, and a light drizzle had begun.

Linton was drinking a scotch on the rocks from the armchair in the office area of the suite. At fifty-two, he was a handsome man. He was tall and lean with short gray hair. He wore an expensive Italian designer suit and a forty-thousand-dollar Rolex.

He had recently divorced his second wife. He'd been courting Diane since his company approached her a few months earlier to run its New York office.

"You going to be all right?" he asked.

Diane nodded. She took a deep breath and another sip of the wine. She set the wine-glass down on a table and removed her suit jacket. She was wearing a translucent white silk blouse. She felt cold without the jacket and rubbed her arms.

"You look great," Linton said. "Goosebumps and all."

"I'll bet," Diane said. She turned to face Linton. "I froze from fear two times on my way over here. The first time was as soon as I was in the car. In our driveway. I couldn't make myself start the car. Then again outside downstairs. I had to go out and smoke to calm myself."

She held out her hands to show him that she was still shaking. "See how calm I am now?"

Linton stood up and removed his suit jacket. He draped it over the back of the chair and made his way to Diane. He put a hand on her shoulder and guided her against him. Diane grabbed his hand with hers and held on tight.

"I almost didn't come," she said. "I was leaving it up to him. He had more important things to take care of."

Linton tried to kiss the back of her neck. Diane pulled away. "I'm sorry," she said. She focused on the traffic on Fifth Avenue. "I'm just nervous. I'll be all right."

Linton moved away. He leaned against the desk and sipped his wine. "Maybe you should have brought your laptop," he said.

Diane smiled. "It is a lot easier for me that way," she said.

"You can save those chats, you know," Linton said. "I've saved a few of ours in the past."

"So have I," Diane said. "I remember the one where you tie me up with my nylons."

"I noticed you wore the white nylons," Linton said.

Diane sipped more wine. Linton made his way over to her again. He kissed her hair. "It's all right," he said. "I'm not rushing you."

He stepped away from her, but Diane held on to his hand. She pulled herself toward him. They held on to each other without speaking. They exchanged a soft kiss. They exchanged another and then another and finally embraced. Diane stepped away to set the wine-glass on the windowsill, taking one last gulp before she embraced Linton again. One of his hands slipped under her skirt, and she darted her tongue deep into his mouth.

* * * * *

"You okay?" Linton asked her.

Diane's head lay against his chest. They had just finished having sex for the first time. Diane was still uncomfortable. She tugged at the sheet to cover her breasts. Linton yawned as he checked his watch. When Diane didn't respond, he repeated his question.

She lit a cigarette and reached out to grab an ashtray from a night table. "I'm fine," she said. "A nervous wreck, but fine."

"You were great," Linton said.

"I was terrified," Diane said.

Linton rubbed her right shoulder. "Not of getting caught, I hope?"

Diane took another drag on the cigarette. "Of everything," she said. "Of being terrible. Of going too far. Of not going far enough. Of not knowing what to do. Everything."

"You were wonderful," he said.

"And, of course," Diane added, "the guilt. I can't help but feel evil now. Except I know when I'm home again, I'll feel the way I did this morning and last night."

"You'll feel worse," Linton said.

"There's always the Internet," Diane said.

"Somehow after today, it won't be the same," Linton said.

Diane played with Linton's chest hairs. "I can't make any promises," she said. "I tried to talk to him about us last night. I told him you were going to be the donor."

"I don't think you should get into me with your husband."

"I had to tell him sooner or later. He knows it's you now. My boss. He doesn't know your name, but he can find that out easy enough."

"That's what I mean," Linton said, suddenly uneasy.

"Eddie's not the type to get jealous," Diane said. "He'll move on. That's his nature."

Linton's face tightened. Diane lit another cigarette. "He wanted to know if we did it," she said. "His face turned red as soon as I mentioned you. That I had a donor. That I was serious."

Linton moved Diane aside so that he could sit up in bed. "That's not a good thing, Diane."

Diane raised herself up on one arm. "What?" she said.

"You're telling your husband way too much about me," he said. "You're baiting him. I think you should go a little easy about this."

Diane squinted. "I'm trying to do the right thing with him," she said. "I don't want to cheat on him, Mike. Trust me, it would be a lot worse if I did that."

Linton made a face. "I don't know that I'm comfortable with a gangster knowing I'm sleeping with his wife."

"You're not sleeping with her," Diane said, somewhat agitated. "You're impregnating her."

"Not just now, we didn't," Linton said.

"I guess not," Diane said. She got up off the bed and wrapped a towel around her body.

Linton stared at her. "I don't want to get into a fight over this, Diane. I'm sorry if I came off the wrong way."

"Eddie isn't a gangster," Diane said. "He's connected."

"I didn't know there was a difference."

"There is a difference," Diane said scornfully. "A big difference. But you needn't worry about him going after you now that he knows about you. He has too much pride. I removed all your risk when I explained it to him."

"I'm sorry, Diane," Linton said.

"Me, too," Diane said. She crushed out her cigarette in the ashtray and made her way to the bathroom.

CHAPTER 13

EDDIE SUCKED IN AIR AS HE LOWERED THE OLYMPIC bar slowly to his chest. He held the weight against his chest a full second before exhaling as he drove the bar straight back up. A growl erupted deep in the back of his throat as three hundred-fifty pounds steadily rose from his chest to where Eddie's elbows locked. He held the weight straight up another full second before racking the bar onto the bench rests.

"How the fuck much was that?" a raspy voice asked from a few feet away.

Eddie sat up on the bench and gathered his breath. He smiled when he saw the short man with a pint-sized orange juice container in his right hand.

"That spiked or you on the wagon?" Eddie asked Joe Sharpetti.

Sharpetti examined his orange juice container a second. "It helps me keep it up," he said.

The two men exchanged a cheek kiss. Sharpetti was a longtime captain with the Vignieri crime family. He had been Eddie Senta's street rabbi back when Eddie thought he wanted to join the Vignieri family.

Eddie had helped save Sharpetti's life once. The gangster had looked out for Eddie ever since.

Sharpetti was a short bulky man. At sixty-two years of age his skin was well tanned but rough. He combed his gray hair straight back. His voice was raspy from forty-five years of smoking.

Eddie pointed at the orange juice. "That's the only thing I ever seen you do in here," he said. "Drink orange juice. I'm surprised they don't call you that, Joey O.J. or something."

Sharpetti sat on the end of the bench Eddie was working on. "You see my girlfriend?" he asked.

Eddie looked around the gym. When he spotted the woman Sharpetti was referring to, he pointed to her. "Talking to that young trainer over there," Eddie said.

Sharpetti stood up to wave at the woman. She was short and muscular and dressed in tight workout attire. Sharpetti stood until she returned his wave. He frowned as he sat on the bench.

"You see her over there with that guy she's with?" he asked Eddie. "You think she's telling that kid how much she loves me, she can't live without me? That cunt. What she's telling him is how much she hates me, she wishes I'd drop dead so she wouldn't have to suck my dick once every couple a weeks, which is what she thinks she has to do now that I put her in the business she always dreamed of. She doesn't have to blow me. What am I some animal's gonna make a broad blow me? But she watches that thing on the HBO and thinks she's a mob whore, and I get a lifeless hummer every two weeks."

Eddie looked at the woman again. "She don't look lifeless to me," he said. "She looks hot. How the hell do you handle something like that?"

Sharpetti waved it off. "I'm at the stage of my life it almost don't make a difference she's hot or not. It's hard enough to deal with the attitude. I gotta' ask her put on that bullshit Indian music they use for the massages they give in here just to drown out the crying routine she goes through."

Sharpetti mimicked a female voice. "'I don't feel right that you come here to the gym. It doesn't look good if the police and the FBI are watching you. I'm afraid I might lose my business.'"

Sharpetti sipped some orange juice, coughed up some phlegm and yawned loud. "Her business," he said. "I take her useless ass off a strip stage and put her in here, in her fucking name, and all she does is show up in tight clothes, and work out, and now it's her business. She ever wakes up and just tells me out right, she don't wanna suck my dick, I think I'll tell her, Oh, is that what you're doing? I couldn't tell."

Eddie smiled. He looked back and forth from Sharpetti to his twenty-six-year-old girlfriend.

"What?" Sharpetti asked.

"I think the two a'you look good together."

"Fuck you, too."

Eddie laughed. "Well, can I ask a question?"

Sharpetti sipped the juice. "Here we go."

"I need a favor," Eddie said.

Sharpetti sipped more orange juice. "What else is new?"

"I want to call in my marker," Eddie said.

"You been calling it in for twelve years now," Sharpetti said.

"I'm serious, Joe," Eddie said. "I want to walk away, give it a shot outside the life."

Sharpetti shrugged. "So walk," he said. "Who the fuck's stopping you?"

"I want to leave my loan book to a friend," Eddie said.

Sharpetti stared at Eddie. "Oh," he said. "I'm your friend. Remember that."

"My other friend," Eddie said. "You know the guy. Tommy Gaetani."

Sharpetti wiped his mouth with a fist. "The guy with the impressions, yeah. The jerk-off I went to bat for how many times with bookies so far? What is this, be kind to a fuck-up week?"

Eddie wiped sweat from his forehead with a towel. "He's a friend from way back," he said. "He's a down-and-out guy."

"And what am I, Santa Claus?"

"I'm only asking because the guy never had any luck."

"He keeps calling bets in and that phenomenon won't change."

Eddie smiled. "Nice word, phenomenon."

Sharpetti toasted Eddie with the orange juice container. "Thank you."

"Tommy ain't a bad guy," Eddie said. "I'm just asking you don't bleed him. We're doing something together end of this week maybe. You'll get a slice of that, too, if it happens."

Sharpetti made a face. "Do I really want to hear this?"

"I'm just saying," Eddie said. "So you don't get nervous when we approach you."

"Do me a favor and approach somebody else," Sharpetti said. "'Specially you bring your friend the comedian, impressionist, whatever the fuck he is."

Eddie started to speak when Sharpetti spoke first. "I guess you don't read the papers," Sharpetti said. "This Jerry Capeci guy, this article he writes, this *Gang Land* thing in *The Daily News*. The guy's got a fuckin' pipeline to the street. Prints shit that's going on as it happens. He knows stuff he can't possibly know without he's got somebody on the inside dropping dimes. I got guys on my crew can't fuckin' wait for Thursday to see if they made his column. This isn't a good thing. All the rest of the crap going on around guys like me, I don't need the extra attention. I don't need to read my name in some newspaper article, this Gang-fuckin'-Land, whatever it is." He stopped to catch his breath. "Used to be a guy could show the colors, have his crew surround him day and night. Not anymore."

Eddie wiped his forehead with a towel. "They keep changing the rules, it won't get any better."

"Tell me about it," Sharpetti said. "Used to be you had to be Sicilian. Then both your parents had to be Italian. Then just the father. Pretty soon, things keep going the way they have, we'll be making anybody ate a slice of pizza."

Eddie smiled. "So, Tommy brings you a cut of this thing we're doing together and a higher percentage of what I give you on the other thing. That okay?"

Sharpetti opened up both his hands to Eddie. "Oh, you want me to kiss your ring finger too while we're at it? I need your permission now? I know what I can do. I can take the entire thing and pay him a hundred a week to pick up envelopes, my friend. I can take the entire thing and tell him to fuck off."

"It would be a favor for a guy who almost took a bullet once," Eddie said.

Sharpetti shook his finger at Eddie. "You distracted the guy, Eddie. You didn't almost take a bullet. Let's not get more dramatic than the HBO here."

Eddie looked up at the ceiling. "Whatever happened to that guy anyway?"

"Very funny," Sharpetti said. He smiled for a second. "A few guys had a talk with him shortly after you distracted his shots and he confessed to who put him up to it."

"That's right," Eddie played. "That was the same week half a crew and a couple of Capos with the Vigneiri's disappeared."

"It was an age of miracles," Sharpetti said. "Something like that."

"And you became street boss shortly thereafter."

"Another one with the HBO."

Eddie handed Sharpetti two hundred-dollar bills. "So this'll be the last one from me."

Sharpetti pocketed the money without looking at it. "With guys like you, guys like me 'll have to work the minimum wage someday."

"What's that under your arms there, Ham or Sirloin?"

"Never mind, wise-ass," Sharpetti said. "You insulted us twice rejecting my offers. Not many guys get to reject the same offer twice the same life. You should be a made guy. Don't forget that, you want to call in favors."

Eddie waved Sharpetti off. "You like me too much, Joe," he said. "You asked because you had to. You didn't really want me involved with your bullshit."

Sharpetti covered his lips with a finger. "Oh, easy, Maverick," he said. "Certain things shouldn't be said out loud, all right?"

"I'll tell Tommy it's three hundred a week," Eddie said. "That fair?"

"Four hundred."

"Three-fifty."

"Three-seventy-five."

"Three-fifty."

Sharpetti showed teeth. "Four hundred."

"Right," Eddie said. "Three-seventy-five."

CHAPTER 14

SINGLETON HUDDLED CLOSE TO THE TABLE ACROSS from the short blonde man who wore an orange prison jumper. They were in a large cafeteria in which long tables were set up in rows with facing metal folding chairs. Uniformed corrections officers were stationed at the head of every other table.

Singleton scratched the right side of his face as he spoke to the blonde man. "I heard you transferred down from upstate," Singleton said. "You lookin' good, Victor. Very good."

"Two more week," Victor Ilynich said. "Maybe one week." He spoke with a pronounced Russian accent. His left hand was bandaged from a recent prison fight in which two bones in the hand were broken.

"Man told me it was more like two days," Singleton said. "Maybe less."

Ilynich shrugged. "I don't think about it," he said.

"So the brothers here treating you good?" Singleton asked.

"Blacks are afraid of accent," Ilynich said.

Singleton raised his eyebrows. "You don't want to go around here talking that trash," he said. "If you know what I mean."

Ilynich shrugged again. "What you are doing here?" he asked.

Singleton sat back on his chair. "That anyway to talk to an old buddy?" he asked. "Man comes to see how a friend is doing, he don't expect the man he coming to see to be rude."

"Please," Ilynich said. "Don't fock with me."

Singleton giggled. "I love the way you people say that word, 'fock.'" He mimicked Ilynich, "Don't fock with me."

Ilynich yawned. "What you want, please?"

"I need to move something," Singleton said, suddenly serious. "Something hot. You mentioned you have a cousin with the Russian mob over in Brooklyn. I'm wondering can he do anything for me?"

"What you moving?" Ilynich asked without looking at Singleton.

"Can't say just yet," Singleton said. "I'm just wondering can your connected cousin do anything for me. You talked enough shit about him upstate. I'm wondering is there anything to your bullshit, or was that all it was, bullshit? There's something in it for you, you weren't stroking me about him."

Ilynich looked away from Singleton.

Singleton rolled his eyes. "Well?"

"Dimi," Ilynich said. "My cousin. If you have something worth something, Dimi can move it for you."

"You sure? You not just saying that now to sound important, I hope? Because you got to know that I know you're nothing more than a fuck-up, Victor. Between upstate and whatever keeps landing you inside, your story is no secret to the world. A fuck-up is a fuck-up is a fuck-up."

"You want help or just to break balls?" Ilynich asked.

Singleton smiled. "That's more like it," he said.

Both men stared hard at each other. Singleton's stare turned to a smirk. Eventually, Ilynich looked away again.

"You got digits I can reach the man at?" Singleton asked. "Your cousin the comrade, I mean. You got a number I can call?"

"I call Dimi," Ilynich said. "He don't take call from you. Not without I talk to him first."

"You got quarters for calls in here?" Singleton asked.

Ilynich opened his hands palms up. Singleton frowned as he pawed five quarters from his front pants pocket. He held them up. "I'll leave these with the man. Use at least one to call your cousin, tell him about me. I don't know when I'll call, but it'll be soon. I need to know I can count on him."

"Dimi is serious," Ilynich said. "Don't fock with him."

Singleton smiled. "There you go again."

"Dimi kill you for pleasure. He don't like black man."

"He never done time, huh?"

Ilynich smirked. "In Russia," he said. "Prison there is real. Prison here is for women."

Singleton ignored that remark. "So he the man, your cousin? That's what you telling me, right? This Dimi motherfucker is the man to see about moving something hot, right?"

Ilynich frowned as he nodded this time.

Singleton glared at Ilynich. "That a real affirmation or you just trying to look important again?"

"You want favor you don't insult me, okay?" Ilynich asked with a sneer.

Singleton nodded. "Fair enough," he said.

"Stupid fock," Ilynich said.

Singleton smiled again.

* * * * *

It took Singleton a little more than forty minutes to get from Riker's Island to Manhattan. He bought a pretzel at a frankfurter stand and waited under the awning of a hair salon.

Singleton watched the ebb and flow of people on Second Avenue.

He watched for women in short skirts and smiled at the ones whom he made eye contact with. After half an hour of women-watching, he saw the man he was waiting for step out of a Yellow cab and wave at Singleton. Special Agent Morris was wearing a suit this time. He carried a black leather briefcase and wore dark wraparound sunglasses.

Singleton had saved a piece of his pretzel. He offered Morris half of it.

"You kidding me?" Morris asked. He lowered the sunglasses he was wearing to eyeball Singleton. "I look that stupid?"

"Only with your shades," Singleton said.

The two men walked north on the west side of Second Avenue until they found a diner. Singleton followed Morris inside and to a booth in the back.

After the waitress set two cups of coffee on their table and took their orders, Morris yawned into a fist. He rubbed his eyes and leaned both arms on the table. He looked into Singleton's eyes as he spoke.

"You been busy, Jimmy?" he asked.

Singleton rolled his eyes.

"We blinked, and your former partner, Ishmael Hawkins, turned up dead," Morris said.

Singleton avoided eye contact as he shuffled two sugar packets. "Jamal," he said. "Had to be."

Morris waited for Singleton to look at him. "Yeah, right," he said. "Same day you met Jamal."

Singleton shook the sugar packets. "Ishmael in a coma, man. What the fuck was he gonna say to hurt me?"

"Consider that brief lapse in our attention your breathing room," Morris said. "Until you have something solid with the comrade."

"And suppose I already have the comrade?" Singleton asked. "What about that?"

Morris rubbed his eyes again. "What about it?"

Singleton furrowed his eyebrows. "I'm here, brother, ain't I? One day you complainin' about me and white women and here I am. Show some interest, my brother. Today I'm here with the Russian you ordered."

Morris looked around the table. "Where?" he asked. "I don't see him?"

Singleton tore open one of the sugar packets and spilled the contents on the table. Morris grabbed one of Singleton's hands to get his attention. "Don't jerk me around, brother," Morris said. "You're here more than a week late. You got your walking papers two weeks ago and I had to reach out to surveillance to learn what you were up to in Harlem."

Singleton looked down at his hand until Morris released it. "Man goes away for two plus years and you gotta ask? Poon, my man. Pussy, what the fuck you think?"

Morris pointed a finger at Singleton. "Surveillance has you on film with a known gunrunner in Harlem," he said. "What's up with that, Jimmy?"

Singleton sat back and smiled. "Somebody feeding you the lingo, huh? You almost sound black you say it that way, 'what's up with that.'"

Morris sipped his coffee. "Your stock is going down fast, my friend," he said as he wiped his mouth with a napkin. "I wouldn't make jokes if I were you."

"I bees a free man, my brother," Singleton said, putting it on. "The white man done made me a deal, and my sentence am officially over."

Morris pushed his coffee aside. He said, "You ignorant motherfucker. You really think what you did, sell out some upstart crackhead nigger moving H for the west side Dominicans, you really think that was enough to shield you the rest of your criminal life?" Morris stopped to crack his knuckles. "First off," he continued, "you didn't deal Jamal away yet. And now your buddy is gone, it looks like you the man on the witness stand after all. Unless you deliver what you started to brag about two minutes ago. Unless you deliver the comrade."

Singleton lost his smile.

"We own you, Jimmy," Morris said. "Never fucking forget that. You our boy. For life. You run that nigga dialogue with somebody wants to hear it. Try it out with MTV, you feel the need to entertain. Or the black network. To me, to your great white Uncle Sam, all you are is a sell-out piece of shit with a long string attached to your rap sheet. I put it out on the street Jimmy Singleton is out and about and on the front line ready to testify against his old employer, Jamal Watkins, your life is over and you know it."

"The fuck you talkin' about?" Singleton asked.

The waitress brought each man a Hamburger Deluxe. Singleton reached for the ketchup. Morris smeared mustard on one side of his hamburger bun.

"The fuck puts mustard on a burger?" Singleton asked, just before he bit into his hamburger.

Morris added a strip of lettuce to his burger. "White boys down at Quantico," he said. "They taught me this and some other things."

Singleton nodded. "Right," he said. "Your wife white, too, right?"

Morris ignored the remark and took a small bite from his burger. "The Russian Dimi Gregov?" he asked as he chewed.

"The fuck I know his last name?" Singleton said. "Dimi. I know him as Dimi. What his fuck-up cousin told me."

"Your cellmate?"

"Yeah, my cellmate," Singleton said. "Ain't that the way you arranged it? Put the brother in the cell with the middle man can lead to the man you want?"

Morris sipped his coffee again. "What do you have, Jimmy? I need to be downtown in half-an-hour."

Singleton jammed some fries into his mouth. "I have a hint of something to do with gold," he said. "South African coins minted from the sweat of the original homeboys."

"Dimi? This from him or Victor?" Morris asked.

Singleton leaned back in the booth as he smirked. "You interested now, though, huh?"

CHAPTER 15

A FEW HOURS AFTER HIS SECOND MEETING WITH THE Special Agent, Singleton went searching for the only man who could ruin the score that Sarah Parker had inadvertently led him to.

Singleton had used a page that he'd torn from a Nassau telephone book to find the address. He was lost for an hour in Great Neck before he finally managed to find the address in Port Washington. He passed the faded blue two-story house twice before driving to a small shopping area set back from the main road a few blocks from Eddie Senta's house.

He ate a bagel with cream cheese and sipped fruit punch in the car that he'd stolen earlier in the day. The loaded .380, minus the two bullets that had killed Ishmael Hawkins the night before, lay under the driver's seat.

Singleton periodically used the pay phone at the gas station on the corner to call Senta's house. When finally he heard a male voice, he immediately hung up. He started the car and drove out of the lot.

It took him less than a minute to get to the address on Fairview Avenue, but when he was just off the corner, Singleton saw a stocky man with dark curly hair leaving the house. It was the same man whom he had spotted in the street outside of Sarah's building. The man Singleton figured was Eddie Senta got into a black Saab parked in the driveway and immediately backed out onto the street. Singleton pulled alongside the curb at the corner. He waited until the Saab was halfway down the block before turning onto the same street to follow it.

He drove carefully as he followed the Saab from several car lengths behind it. The Saab took him back to the Long Island Expressway, then the Cross Island Parkway, and finally the Belt Parkway. Thirty-five minutes later, Singleton followed it to a small house in Canarsie, Brooklyn.

The guy Singleton figured was Eddie Senta went into the house. He reached down to grab the gun, but a group of kids started to toss a football further up the street. He was forced to wait a full fifteen minutes before Senta left the house. A tall kid with curly hair was with him. Singleton watched as they drove off. He checked his watch and cursed to himself.

He thought of his own childhood as he watched the man drive away with the kid. An aunt had raised Singleton after his mother died of an overdose. He had been beaten by two of his aunt's boyfriends. He had dropped out of high school in his sophomore year and was arrested seven times before his seventeenth birthday.

He had a son somewhere himself, but Singleton wasn't sure if the mother had moved down south or was still hooking in the South Bronx. He had never tried to find out, and he never would. Life was hard enough without the baggage.

Brakes screeched in the distance, bringing him back to the matter at hand. Except for the dynamics, this wasn't unlike the first time that Singleton had killed a man. Back then, it was another mugger who had arbitrarily trespassed on his score. Now Singleton was the odd man in.

Eddie Senta was the mark, the person between Singleton and fifteen thousand dollars cash.

He frowned as he watched the Saab turn left at the corner at the end of the block. He drove the stolen car another few blocks to a parking lot near the train station that he remembered was the last stop on the "L" line. Singleton stood with the door open and relieved himself on the front seat and floor of the stolen car and then made his way the few blocks to the train station. He bought himself *The Daily News* and another container of fruit punch. He smoked a cigarette outside of the station before going in to take a seat for the ride back to Manhattan.

* * * * *

Jack Senta, at six-foot-three, was tall for his fifteen years. He was a dark-complexioned boy with dark curly hair and dark eyes. Except for his height and slimness, Jack looked a lot like his father. Lately, also like his father when he was in high school, Jack had started to cut his woodshop classes. Eddie Senta was there to talk about a punishment.

"I called to remind you last night," Jack said to his father. "I didn't try to avoid it."

They were walking around the half-mile circle in Seaview Park in Canarsie, Brooklyn. It had stopped raining a few minutes earlier. Jack was wearing a Buffalo Bills football sweatshirt with a hood. Eddie was in a black sweatshirt jacket. Father and son had to sidestep some of the puddles in the worn track as they strolled.

"I appreciate the call," Eddie said. "Of course, it did come a few days after the call your mother made."

Jack shrugged. "I took a shot," he said.

Eddie laughed.

"I hate woodshop," Jack said. "It sucks."

Eddie let the silence of the moment unease his son.

"I know I have to go, but I still hate it," Jack said. "And I'm doing great in everything else."

"You're doing good in everything else," Eddie corrected him. "But you can't cut woodshop."

"Let's face it, Dad. I'm not going into construction," Jack said.

"What the hell do you do when you're cutting woodshop anyway? Hang out with the guys smoking weed?"

Jack made a face. "Nice try, Dad," he said. Eddie laughed. "I won't skip it again," he added.

Eddie nodded. They both walked to one side to avoid a huge puddle. Eddie nudged his son with an elbow.

"What?" Jack asked.

"The cost of skipping," Eddie said. "I mean, it's cute and all, your telling me about it, your promise not to do it again and all, but there still has to be a price, no?"

Jack rolled his eyes. "Don't make me read some dumb book again," he pleaded. "It's almost the end of the semester. I have finals in like a few weeks."

Eddie draped his right arm around his son's shoulders. "I was thinking more in terms of those old baseball articles you used to write for me way back."

Jack made a face. "Are you serious?"

"Yeah," Eddie laughed. "The ones you used to write for your allowance."

"And for punishment," Jack said.

"Whatever."

"Don't you think I'm a little old to play *Strat-O-Matic* baseball again? How am I supposed to write an article without playing?"

Eddie veered his son away from another big puddle. "It doesn't have to be *Strat-O-Matic*. You could do it on something else. Whatever you want. Some current event thing."

Jack was shaking his head. "Great. I already have to do that for my social studies class. We're doing unions now. My teacher loves unions. We're supposed to write an essay about that now."

"You're a little young, but how do you feel about them?" Eddie asked.

"I don't know. I know you're not crazy about them."

"I used to be. I was a window cleaner for a few years. Remember? That was a union job. I loved unions back then. It depends on which side of the fence you're on. On whose ox is gored."

"Huh?" Jack said.

"Well, look what they did to sports, the unions. They got too full of themselves. They got greedy and ruined everything. Write a paper on how much more it costs to go to a baseball game today because of the unions. I remember my father took me to see Willie Mays at Shea Stadium it cost three-fifty for a box seat. Three dollars and fifty cents, not three hundred fifty dollars."

Jack pleaded with his father. "Please don't make me do another union paper. I don't care about that stuff."

"All right, all right, so it doesn't have to be on unions, what you write for me," Eddie said. "Save the antiunion essay for your teacher. How about something going on in your life right now? Or maybe something about you and your friends."

"Right," Jack said. "You want me to confess in a paper to some shit I'm doing with my friends. Another nice try."

Eddie ruffled his son's hair. "I took a shot," he said.

* * * * *

Near the end of their walk together, Eddie stuffed three fifty-dollar bills into his son's front pants pocket. "That's for your mother," he said. "You get ten from that. After you finish that paper."

"I'm really getting too old for that stuff," Jack told his father. "Writing reports for allowance is old, Dad."

Eddie kissed his son's head. "Yeah, and my mother used to make me listen to opera, read the librettos, and then write reports on them. Like book reports, only it was opera. I hated opera. But I had to do it. And it isn't for allowance, pal. It's for punishment."

Jack looked down at the ground.

"What's wrong?" Eddie asked.

"You ever like the opera after she made you do all that shit? Ah, I mean crap."

Eddie frowned at his son. "You meant shit," he said. "No, I didn't. I do remember some of the stories, though, from reading the librettos. And every once in a while I hear something on the radio I recognize. I guess that isn't so bad, right? At least it makes me think about my mother."

"So someday when I'm torturing my own kid I guess I can tell him how you tortured me and how I have good memories of it because I was being punished?"

Eddie play-slapped the back of his son's head. "Wiseass," he said.

"Grandma ever take you to an opera?"

Eddie rolled his eyes. "No, thank God," he said. "But she threatened to plenty of times. Maybe I should do the same with you, eh?"

"I'm not too crazy about baseball," Jack said. "Especially those stupid playoffs. You could always take me to a playoff game for punishment."

"Very cute, kid," Eddie said.

"I took another shot," Jack said.

* * * * *

When Eddie dropped off his son for the day, he reminded Jack about the money that he had given him. "I want that report before you take the ten, pally," he said.

"Why do you want them?" Jack asked. "Do you really read them?"

"Every single one," Eddie said. "I have almost all of the torture papers you did for me. I'm saving them for my grandchildren."

Jack held up both his hands. "I'm not putting my kids through that," he said.

"Yes, you will," Eddie said. "Same as I did."

"No way," Jack said.

"Listen," Eddie said, leaning into his son for a hug. "I'm getting out of that other thing I do."

"Serious?"

"Yes."

"Why?"

"A lot of reasons," Eddie said. "I'm done with it, for one thing. I don't need it anymore. It served its purpose."

"You going to stick with the computers?"

"Maybe," Eddie said. "I was thinking about a pizza parlor."

Jack was surprised. "Really?"

"Maybe, I don't know yet. There's no rush. I just wanted to tell you I'm finished with that other shit. I know you're not enamored with it the way some kids are. I tried to make sure of that. I'm glad you never looked at it that way."

"I just figured you did what you had to do," Jack said.

"Well, I did it and now it's over," Eddie said. "Like you and no more cutting woodshop, understand?"

Jack was smiling again. "Yeah, I guess."

Eddie kissed his son on the forehead. "Good boy," he said. "Now get started on that paper. Three pages on any opera of your choice."

"What?" Jack asked.

"You heard me," Eddie said. "In memory of my mother. Three pages, single-spaced, on any opera you want."

"I don't want to listen to an opera," Jack said. "Or read one."

Eddie winked at his son. "That's the entire idea behind torture, my son," he said. "To get you to do something you don't want to do."

"That's great, Dad," Jack said. "Thanks a lot."

Eddie winked again. "You're welcome," he said. "Anytime."

CHAPTER 16

THE STREET ON WHICH TOMMY GAETANI LIVED IN Corona, Queens, was a row of brick attached and semi-attached two- and three-family houses. Tommy's house had a garage that barely accommodated his Toyota Camry. As Eddie parked across the street from Tommy's house, he noticed the Lincoln Town Car had been backed into the garage. Tommy's familiar black Camry was parked directly in front of the house.

Eddie looked up and down the street as he got out of his car. This was an active block. A group of young kids played Wiffle ball under a streetlight, while a group of women watched from a small terrace across the street. Eddie took his time getting the duffle bag from the backseat of his car. When he looked up, Tommy was at the top of the stairs.

"How the fuck you get that thing in there?" Eddie asked, pointing at the nose of the Lincoln Town Car sticking out of the garage.

"It wasn't easy," Tommy said.

They squeezed their way alongside the car to the back of the garage.

"You ready to make a pass?" Eddie asked. He was wearing a dark gray sports jacket, black slacks, and a white shirt with a blue tie hanging around the open collar. Tommy was dressed in black slacks, a light blue shirt, a navy tie, and black shoes. He held a gray sports jacket folded over his right forearm.

"I could hardly stop thinking about this," he said. "Yeah, I'm ready. Ready as I'll ever be."

Eddie set the duffel on the edge of the trunk. "Good," he said. "Everything we need is in there. Wire cutters, screwdrivers, box cutters. We'll do a dry run tonight to prep for tomorrow. I'd like to watch the office lights tonight, see what time they go off. Exactly what time."

Tommy made a face when Eddie dropped the duffel into the trunk. A heavy thud caught Tommy's attention. "What was that?" he asked.

"A crowbar," Eddie said.

Both men double-checked each other. "Nice touch, the white shirt," Tommy told Eddie.

"I have to make sure I don't spill nothing on this because my wife assured me I don't have another one," Eddie said. "It's my interviewing shirt."

"Same here," Tommy said. "I didn't think to look until it was time to get dressed. It's the only shirt I had in the closet still fits, so we better go tomorrow. Between your wardrobe and mine, we'll reek in two days."

"This where we storing the computers?" Eddie asked.

"Until I get them over to Brooklyn," Tommy said. "Unless we go there first. We can. I have a key. My friend has a driver who gets around. Good hustler. He can probably get rid of whatever we have by the end of next week. He's got some Irishman over in Sunnyside, Queens, moves swag all the time. My friend said the guy's taking orders already."

Eddie checked the trunk once more before squeezing out of the garage. Tommy slipped his way inside of the car by way of the driver's door and started the engine. He eased out of the garage slowly. Eddie jumped in when the back of the car cleared the end of the garage.

Tommy got out of the car to close and lock the garage door. When he sat back behind the wheel, he saw that Eddie was sipping a Diet Coke that he'd found in the cup holder.

Tommy pointed to the can. "No, Eddie, uh, that's at least two hours old," he said.

Eddie drained the can and set it back in the cup holder. "Yuck!" he said. "That taste like shit."

"That's the other thing," Tommy said.

"What?" Eddie said. He was wiping his tongue with his fingers.

Tommy made a face.

"What?" Eddie repeated.

"I used it for an ashtray," Tommy said.

"Fuck!" Eddie yelled. He wiped his tongue with a paper napkin that he found in the dashboard. "Jesus Christ, Tommy!"

* * * * *

The traffic on Corona Avenue was heavy because of an accident. Tommy grew impatient and tried to veer around a UPS delivery truck, but oncoming traffic quickly blocked him. He took a long drag on his cigarette and opened his window to let the smoke escape.

"I got some good news for you," Eddie said. "Whatever happens tonight."

"I can use it," Tommy said. He was still struggling to see around the UPS truck directly ahead of him.

"I'm putting my book up for sale," Eddie said. "Fifty cents on the dollar. Same as the wiseguy's pay."

"Hey, I wish I had it, the fifty cents," Tommy said. "What the fuck!" he yelled out of the window.

Eddie put a hand on Tommy's shoulder. "Relax," he said. "We have plenty of time. We make a stop in Richmond Hill and we'll head back to get in position. We're gonna wait on Jackson Avenue. It's all back and forth, and it's just a practice run. There's no rush."

Tommy let out a deep breath. "If you say so."

"Anyway, you do have the fifty cents," Eddie said. "You can pay it off as you collect. I'll take you around, introduce you to my people. You won't have much trouble with it. Most of it is solid. There's always the one or two jerks, the ones you have to chase, stay on top of, but it's a solid book. You'll pay it off in a year or so. Less if you're determined."

Tommy looked surprised. "Geez, Eddie, you sure you wanna go that route?"

Eddie nodded. "Pretty sure," he said. "It's not like I can't change my mind later on and start over. I can always put money out. I can always run another sheet. Somebody will always come up with a score from somewhere. I figure I'll never know for sure until I give it a try, whether or not I can live without this anymore. You know what I mean? Sometimes we get stuck in what we do. The comfort of it. And we never let go. I don't want to hang on for the wrong reasons."

Tommy was shaking his head. "It's a lot of scratch to give up, Eddie," he said. "I mean, I hope this ain't Diane talking here, what you just said. It's like these legit guys give up a perfectly good business to go live in the fucking woods. I hope that's not where you're heading with this. On account of Diane, I mean. If her flaky shit finally got to you or something. Because I gotta tell you, one friend to another, no broad is worth that kind of transformation, buddy. I mean, you do have the ability to work two worlds at the same time and all, but the bottom line is, both those worlds are here in the big city. Not out in the fucking wilderness someplace. I just don't see you up in the mountains, chopping fucking wood, building a fireplace, planting fucking seed, or whatever the fuck those guys do up there. I don't see you doing that bullshit at all."

Eddie smiled. "You finished?" he asked.

Tommy played with his mustache. "What?"

"I said I want to give going legit a shot," Eddie said. "I'm not joining no commune."

Tommy glanced quickly at Eddie. "Oh, okay. You're smart to wait out having the kid."

"A kid?" Eddie asked.

Tommy squinted, trying to figure it out. "Huh?" he said.

Eddie was smiling at Tommy as he leaned away from him.

"I don't know," Tommy said. "I'm all fucking confused here."

Traffic finally started to move again. Tommy veered off Corona Avenue and used side streets to get to the Grand Central Parkway. He moved to the center lane as soon as he cleared the Parkway traffic. "What's the book worth, Eddie? Net, I mean."

"Twelve hundred a week, most weeks," Eddie said. "Sometimes more, sometimes less. You know how that goes. Joe Sharp's cut is three-seventy-five a week. And don't forget that. Especially up front, don't forget it."

"Wow," Tommy said. "I won't be dealing direct with Joe, will I?"

"Not for a while you won't," Eddie said.

"I know he was pissed backing off those bookies the last few times," Tommy said.

Eddie nodded. "Yes, he was. So you can't get into it again and expect help. And you can't jerk around while you're picking up shy money. The way it works, with Joe Sharp, you don't fuck up, Tommy. Not more than once in some instances. You've already run your limit with him, trust me. This thing will only work if you do the right thing. By yourself and by me. So lay off the bets until you lay some road under your feet. Show the man something before you need him for another favor. In fact, do yourself one better and never reach out for help. It's the favors in this life wind up coming back to haunt us."

Tommy nodded.

"The other thing," Eddie continued. "It be a good idea you give him a cut of this thing we're doing. If the money is there."

"Who do I deal with?"

"Probably one of his guys at the strip joint on Queens Boulevard,

Bella Bambina," Eddie said. "You show up and quietly ask for Joe Sharp, you have something for him. The word will get to whoever is sitting the joint, and they'll approach you for Joe. I'll introduce you to the guys next week. Do yourself a big favor, and don't spend any extra time around there. You need to look at naked broads, buy yourself a *Playboy*. The exposure from that place is nothing but bad. It's a known hangout. You'll be on videotape from the first time you walk in."

"Done," Tommy said. "You sure you don't mind I don't have a dime up front?" he asked. "I'd understand if you wanted to dump the thing for the cash up front. I know I would."

"Let's see how it goes," Eddie said. "You pay up ten, say, and decide you can't do the rest, you'll have twenty large on the street. I'll feed them to you, the customers, as you pay them down."

"I can't tell you how much I appreciate it, what you're doing," Tommy said. "Serious."

Eddie playfully punched Tommy on the right leg. "Well, better you than some wiseguy got his button through bloodlines."

Tommy lit a cigarette and did a Richard Nixon impersonation. "Ah, Spiro? Are you really going legit? All the way legit?"

Eddie laughed. "I'm gonna give it a try," he said.

"Good for you," Tommy said, still doing Nixon.

Eddie belched into a fist. "Every once in a while I used to think about going into business for myself. The computers, for one thing. Or a pizza place. I always wanted a pizza place."

Tommy was smiling from ear to ear. "Good for you," he said, dropping the Nixon impersonation. "Really."

"Imagine," Eddie said. "Me in a pizza joint? I'd weigh four hundred pounds."

Tommy shot Eddie a wink. "It's a cash business, so it can't be all bad," he said. "Be a nice change, too, an Italian owning a pizza joint. Instead of all the Indians and Dominicans with the accents." Tommy did an Indian accent. "Forrr dollar, please. And would you like a stick of incense?"

Eddie laughed again. "We'll see," he said.

Tommy took a turn punching Eddie. "Maybe you need another sign from God," he said.

"Maybe," Eddie said.

Shea Stadium was on their left, across the Grand Central Parkway. Eddie was looking at the neon lighting on the façade. "Well, whatever you do," Tommy said, "I appreciate everything. You're still my hero."

Eddie looked away from the stadium. "Yeah, well, let's get through tonight and tomorrow night before we celebrate," he said. "Then we can plan a fucking parade."

CHAPTER 17

A T NINE O'CLOCK THE SAME NIGHT, SARAH PAGED Eddie Senta to let him know about a change in plans. She dialed his pager several times in a row, each time adding her coded identification number and 9-1-1 to let him know that it was an emergency.

After fifteen minutes or so, Eddie called the office telephone number.

"Hello!" Sarah said, unable to restrain her anxiety.

"What's up?" Eddie asked.

"It's tonight," Sarah said.

"Shit," Eddie said. "What time?"

"Sometime after midnight. He wasn't specific, but he's at the airport with his wife. Some emergency. She's going to see her sister in Miami. I was told to meet Larry and Ivan at the storage apartment on the next block after one o'clock. It's where he keeps the office supplies and his hideaway bedroom. On Thirty-first Street."

"Does he have that other thing with him?" Eddie asked.

"I don't know," Sarah said. "But the cleaning people are here after midnight. If he gets it before they leave, there's nothing you can do."

"What about on the street?" Eddie asked.

"What?" Sarah said, somewhat shocked. "Oh, God, it's crowded here, Eddie. You know that. Thirty-fourth Street and Park?"

Eddie remained silent.

"Eddie?" Sarah said.

"Can you take a look-see while you're there? Is it safe?"

"The drawer is locked," Sarah said. "I already checked it."

Eddie was silent again.

"Maybe you want to wait and see," Sarah said. "Maybe do it tomorrow night?"

Eddie was still silent.

"Eddie?" Sarah said.

"This have anything to do with your new friend?" he asked.

"No, damn it," Sarah said. "How can you even think that?"

Eddie was silent again.

"Well?" Sarah asked.

"I don't know yet," Eddie said. "I'll have to think about it."

"Do you want me to page you when I know they're not at the office?" Sarah asked, somewhat annoyed. "When we get to the storage apartment, I can give you a call from my cell phone. I'll beep your pager."

"What time is maintenance usually gone by?" Eddie asked.

"Two o'clock, I think," Sarah said. "I've been up there with Larry after two, and they were already gone. But you can tell from the street if you want. They usually turn off the office lights when they leave, and they have to exit from the Thirty-second Street door. There's no other way out."

"Okay," Eddie said. "Punch in a bunch of fives. That'll mean it's clear from your boss walking in. We'll watch the door ourselves."

"Okay," Sarah said.

"Later," Eddie said.

"Eddie?" Sarah said, but Eddie had already hung up.

* * * * *

"What was that all about?" Tommy asked Eddie. They were parked on Jackson Avenue in Queens. Tommy was lighting a cigarette. Eddie immediately lit one of his own after turning off the power on his cell telephone.

"I don't know yet," Eddie said.

"That the girl?"

"Yeah," Eddie said. He took a few drags on his cigarette.

"And?"

"They're doing the deal tonight," Eddie said. "Sometime after mid-night, but she isn't exactly sure. Which doesn't give us much time to get in and out, whether or not the money is still there. We got the cleaning crew to consider, too. Or we can wait until later, or tomorrow, and hope they didn't do the deal yet. Maybe he just goes to see what he's buying first. Maybe they make the exchange tomorrow night."

"That's a lot of maybe's," Tommy said.

Eddie nodded. "Tell me about it."

* * * * *

James Singleton heard the sound of the apartment door open and close. He listened as the locks were engaged and heard the voices of two men as well as Sarah's. He was in the closet in the back bedroom, holding the .380 in his right hand. He folded the small couch pillow he had brought from the living room under his left arm as he slowly made his way to the doorway leading to the apartment hallway.

Singleton waited a few minutes while the party took turns using the bathroom. When he was sure Sarah was in the bathroom, he leaned to one side of the bedroom doorway to listen for conversation coming from the living room.

* * * * *

When she was finished dressing, Sarah applied a fresh coat of red lipstick. She slipped on black heels and pulled up her nylons, clipping them into her garter belt snaps. She stood up straight, facing the mirror.

Sarah closed her eyes and took deep breaths. She thought about a beach. She pictured herself and Singleton sipping drinks under an umbrella. She pictured them making love in the water. She imagined them living together.

Opening her eyes, she was startled at the sight of herself in the mirror. Her gaze was drawn to her red lips. She felt a sudden chill and looked away. Adjusting her nylons one last time, she flushed the toilet, ran her fingers under warm water, and opened the door.

* * * * *

"Sarah's amazing, Ivan, wait and see," Singleton heard one man say.

"She has a very big chest," the other man said.

"Wait until you see them in the flesh," the first man said. "Great big tits."

Both men giggled.

Singleton could hear the toilet flush in the bathroom. He heard the water run a few seconds before the door opened. He stood in the shadow of the bedroom door to watch the apartment hallway. He could see Sarah's shadow on the far wall. He peeked into the hallway and saw that she was dressed in a black garter belt and nylons, a bra, and high heels.

"Good girl," he whispered to himself.

"Wow!" he heard both men say.

"What did I tell you?" said the man whom Singleton figured for Sarah's boss.

"She's beautiful!" the other man said. "You're beautiful!"

"Thanks," he heard Sarah say.

"Why don't you sit over there next to Ivan," the boss said. "Get comfortable with each other while I look something over."

"You really are beautiful," the man, Ivan, kept telling Sarah.

* * * * *

Singleton could see the shadow cast by Sarah's boss as he leaned over and opened a black bag. The man picked up the bag and sat in the single armchair in the living room. Singleton counted to ten and started down the hallway. He was fully inside of the room when Sarah's boss finally looked up at him. Using the pillow as a muffler, he fired two shots into Larry Singotti's chest. Singotti collapsed in the armchair. The black bag and several Krugerrands dropped from his lap onto the floor.

The man on the couch sat up straight at the sound of the muffled gun. Sarah fell off his lap onto the floor directly in front of the couch.

Singleton waved the gun at Sarah for her to move to one side. Her eyes were wide open in terror. She crawled away from the man on the couch as Singleton moved in closer. The man gasped as he held up both hands in front of his face and twisted up one leg in a futile attempt to block the shots. Two of the three shots made it through the barrier of shaking limbs and entered his chest. The third shattered the bone in his upraised leg but the man never felt it.

Sarah was backing away from the couch an inch at a time on the floor. She struggled to stand up. She was trembling wildly. She waved her hands at the gun as Singleton shook his head.

"I'm sorry, baby," he said. "But you were right about you and men and bad relationships. You one unlucky bitch."

Sarah started to scream, but the bullet from the first shot exploded into her chest. She was thrown back hard against the wall, her body slumping as a second and then a third shot entered her stomach. Blood flowed from her mouth as her body rested on the floor, and her head tilted to one side in death.

* * * * *

She had been on the fringe of shock when she saw Singleton shoot her boss. It was happening, but it wasn't happening. He was suddenly there in the room, and the sound of the gun, like a firecracker in a hallway, made her jump.

When Singleton motioned for her to get out of the way, Sarah reacted from instinct and crawled. Her eyes were focused on his. She could feel her heart beating, but she had stopped breathing. She saw Ivan's body jerk from the concussion of the bullets. She could see his blood stain his clothes. She could see the life leaving his body.

When Singleton turned to her, his final words were no more humiliating than how she was dressed, she was thinking. The last thought that she had before her new boyfriend killed her was, "How silly I'll look when they find me."

* * * * *

The clip had one more bullet in it. Singleton stepped up to Sarah's boss and held the barrel of the gun against his right temple. He remembered the pillow and used it again to muffle the shot. The pillow deflected the bullet off to the left, where it passed through his right eye and into his brain.

Singleton quickly gathered the coins that had fallen to the floor. He looked inside of the bag that contained the gold and his eyes opened wide. He spotted the second bag alongside a small coffee table and grabbed it, looking inside. His eyes opened even wider. "Yeah, baby," he whispered to himself. "Motherfuckin' lotto."

CHAPTER 18

EXCEPT FOR THE HALLWAY LIGHTS, THE OFFICES OF Larry Singotti and Associates were dark. Once they were inside, Eddie and Tommy had ninety seconds to input the security code before the alarm sounded. Eddie punched in the four numbers and turned the hallway lights on.

Tommy set the dolly on the floor and followed Eddie around the corner toward one end of the office. Eddie found the corner office's door open. He switched on the lights and headed straight for the large oak desk across the room. He opened the duffel and pulled out the crowbar.

Eddie used the crowbar to break the lock on the top drawer in Larry Singotti's desk. The drawer splintered around the lock. Eddie pulled it open to find an empty manila envelope with writing across the top. He frowned at the characters he noticed first: "15K."

"Shit," he said.

"Maybe it's in another drawer," Tommy said.

"Maybe," Eddie said.

The two men riffled through the side drawers of the big oak desk.

None of them were locked, but there was no cash to be found. Tommy went through a few of the cabinets in the wall unit, while Eddie emptied the drawers of a long bureau behind the desk.

"Fuck," Eddie said, after spilling the contents of the last drawer on the floor. "He must have taken it already."

"Unless they didn't do the deal yet," Tommy said. "Maybe the guy took it home with him."

Eddie was thinking out loud. "He wouldn't want his wife to know about it," he said. "Sarah said the money would be in the top drawer."

"Maybe we should've come earlier?" Tommy asked.

Eddie shook his head. "The maintenance crew," he said. "They didn't finish until after one. Sarah said something about an emergency. The guy took his wife to the airport or something. They probably made the switch right after that, after he dropped his wife off. We had to wait for the cleaning crew to leave anyway."

"Maybe the gold is here," Tommy said.

Eddie shook his head again. "Sarah said he's got this other office he uses for supplies. Some apartment in a building nearby here. He probably left it over there until Monday, until he can put it in a safe deposit box or something."

"Fuck," Tommy said. "What do you want to do?"

"Get out of here," Eddie said. "Except I don't like taking risks like this for the sake of pissing myself off. Let's get the computers, whatever the fuck we can carry, and get lost."

* * * * *

Twenty minutes later, Eddie slammed shut the trunk of the Lincoln Town Car and sat in the backseat as he set four laptop computers on the floor of the car. Tommy put the car in drive, and they headed east on Thirty-second Street. At the end of the block, Tommy turned right onto Lexington Avenue.

"You really think they already did the deal?" Tommy asked.

Eddie was biting his lower lip. "Either that or somebody got there first," he said. "Somebody with a key for the lock in that top drawer."

"That third party you mentioned?"

"I don't know. I hope not."

"You want to stop by, see if your friend is home? Maybe ask her direct, see what she knows?"

"Not with this shit in the car, no," Eddie said. "Let's just dump this stuff off for now." He was looking at the laptop computers that he had stacked on the floor. "I don't know how many PC towers we got in the trunk, but I have four laptops back here with me," Eddie said.

"And two up here makes six, makes an even dozen with the ones in the trunk," Tommy said. "The ones without the screens and stuff. That ain't so bad, right?"

"It's better than coming out with our dicks in our hands," Eddie said.

Tommy looked at Eddie in the rearview mirror. "Except maybe your friend is thinking that way, too. At least they got the computers. Is that what you're thinking now? Maybe she decided a third wasn't enough after all."

Eddie stared at Tommy in the mirror. "I don't know what to think," he said.

CHAPTER 19

I T WAS FOUR-THIRTY IN THE MORNING, NEARLY FORTY hours since she'd last seen her husband, when Diane Senta returned home. The house was dark. She noticed Eddie's Saab parked in the driveway. She removed her shoes as soon as she stepped inside of the house. She climbed the stairs on tiptoes and noticed that the light in the empty bedroom they used as an office was on. She peaked inside and saw that Eddie had been on the computer. His AOL logon screen was still up.

Diane used the bathroom to change her clothes. When she was finished, she carefully opened the bedroom door. She tiptoed her way around the room to pull the sheets down on the bed. Eddie lay on his side facing away from her. When she was finally settled in bed, Eddie lit a match and put it to a cigarette.

"You're up?" Diane asked.

"I guess it's my turn, huh," Eddie said.

"Why didn't you say something?" Diane asked. She turned over in the bed. "I was tiptoeing all over the place."

"It's four-thirty in the morning," Eddie said.

"I know," Diane said.

"You didn't come home last night," Eddie said.

"I know," Diane repeated.

"You think you could've called?"

Diane lit a cigarette.

"Well?" Eddie said. "We gonna play this game much longer, or you gonna tell me where the fuck you been?"

Diane sat up in the bed. Eddie remained on his side. He reached out to flick the ash off his cigarette into the ashtray on his night table.

"I was out," Diane said.

"Oh," Eddie said, "I know you were out. Where were you out?"

Diane turned in the bed to face Eddie. "It's what I wanted to talk to you about the other night," she said.

Now Eddie sat up. "You started to tell me you were gonna fuck your boss," he said. "In fact, that's exactly what you said. You were gonna fuck your boss in order to get pregnant by a Ph.D. likes to run."

"Please, Eddie."

"Well?"

"What?"

"Did you?" Eddie asked, his arms out to his sides. "Is that where you were the last couple days?"

Diane took a long drag on her cigarette. "Yes," she said finally.

Eddie stared at her for a moment. He took a deep breath and punched the bed hard. "Jesus fucking Christ," he said finally and then turned away from her.

"I want you to listen to me," Diane said. "I need you to listen to me, Eddie."

Eddie remained silent. His body was tense. He gripped the sheets.

Diane nervously lit another cigarette. She took several drags before she could speak again. "I made a mistake," she said. "Yesterday, with Mike. I . . . ."

Eddie wheeled on her in the bed. He leaned over and pointed a finger in her face. "I don't want to hear his fucking name!" he yelled.

Diane jumped from Eddie's outburst. She dropped her cigarette and had to scramble to find it. "Shit," she said. "You scared me."

Eddie glared at her. He held the stare until his jaw hurt from clenching his teeth.

Diane started over. "I made a mistake," she said. "And I'm sorry I hurt you. I'm sorry I hurt myself, believe me. I was too anxious. I needed some kind of response, I think. From you, Eddie. I think that's why I did this."

Eddie made a face. "For attention, Diane?" he asked with sarcasm.

"Yes," Diane said. "In some ways, yes. And because I want something you won't give me."

"Yeah, well, you can write off having my kid as a dead-and-buried issue now, I'll tell you that much," Eddie said.

"I know," Diane said. "I understand that. But I still want a baby, Eddie. And I know we'll split up over this. Maybe we would have anyway. I made a mistake about who I chose and the method. I should have gone about it differently."

Eddie got out of bed and lit a cigarette. "If you wanted to know if the prick was serious or not, you should have told him you wanted his sperm in a test tube," he said.

"Maybe," Diane said.

"Don't take me for a fool, Diane," Eddie continued. "You went to bed with this guy because you wanted to. I know how it works, trust me."

"Yes," Diane said, "I was curious. You're right. He flirted with me. He told me how pretty I looked. That I was sexy. That . . . ."

Eddie pointed a finger in her face again. "I'm not one of your fucking colleagues in therapy, so don't tell me the fucking details!" he yelled.

Diane jumped back. Eddie crushed out his cigarette and tossed it across the room. "You understand me?" he yelled. He waited for Diane to nod. "You feel you need to tell someone, call your fuckin' therapist and lay it on her. Or go on your computer and log on to AOL. Me? I'm not interested in any of the fucking details of how or why or when my wife fucked her boss, okay? Under-fucking-stand? Clear enough?"

Diane waited for Eddie to light a fresh cigarette. "I had to do this," she said. "No matter what happens to us. I think I had to. . . ."

"And I'm real fucking glad for you," Eddie said. "You broke new ground. You're growing. One for your therapist."

A few moments of silence passed between them.

"We've been distant, Eddie," Diane said. "We've been distant a long time now."

Eddie was shaking his head. "Then you leave me," he said. "You separate or divorce me, but you don't run off and fuck some guy because we're distant. Or was this phase one of your plan to have kids without me? Did you protect yourself, or was last night the big night?"

Diane lowered her head. "I didn't get pregnant," she said.

"So it was just a bullshit story," Eddie said. "The pregnancy thing. That was just bullshit, too?"

"No," Diane said. "I was serious. I'm still serious. We just thought it would be better to wait."

"Get some practice in?" Eddie asked sarcastically. "That his idea? The genius from California? No wonder he's the fuckin' boss."

"I didn't know how to start talking to you," Diane said.

Eddie held a hand up. "Please, Diane, don't even bother trying to explain this to me. You did what you had to do. Fine. I'll deal with it."

Diane was pleading with him now. "I know it was wrong," she said. "I wanted to tell you about him, how close we were to going through with it. I wanted to tell you. I started to tell you the other night. You didn't want to hear it. I was serious, Eddie."

Eddie wheeled on her again. "Bullshit!" he yelled. "Or you would have talked to me. You wanted to do what you did more, Diane. Or you would have talked to me. Understand? That's how it works. You do what you want to do. We all do."

Diane let a moment pass. "I'm sorry," she said.

Eddie was looking into her eyes. "Do you love him?" he asked.

Diane gasped. "No, of course not."

Eddie glared at her again. "Why not? You fucked him, didn't you? You're going to carry his kid."

"Eddie, please."

He held up both hands. "Right, right, I'm sorry," he said. "I really don't want to know the details. I really don't." He crushed out another cigarette. "If you want out, Diane, then do it," he said. "Just don't make an asshole out of me. I don't do it to you. I've never cheated on you."

"How am I supposed to know that?" Diane asked.

"Because I'm telling you, that's how!" Eddie yelled. He threw a pillow across the room at the blinds. "Bitch!" he screamed. "Because I just fuckin' told you so!"

Diane remained motionless on the bed, waiting for Eddie's color to return to normal. "What happens now?" she asked finally.

"We'll do what we have to do," Eddie said. Emotionally exhausted, he collapsed against the headboard. "Just like everybody else in the world," he said. "We'll do what we have to do."

CHAPTER 20

Detective Alex Pavlik stretched his long arms over his head on the street outside of the city morgue. He was a tall, imposing man at six-foot-three. His hands were rough from several years of both amateur and professional boxing. Most of the knuckles on both hands had been broken at one time or another. His nose had been broken seven times.

Pavlik was waiting for his partner. They had been assigned to a triple homicide in the early morning. Now it was nearly eight o'clock, and Pavlik wanted to get home. His partner was still in the morgue asking questions whose answers Pavlik wasn't interested in knowing.

He lit a cigarette to kill the time. He'd finished four cigarettes before his partner was back out on the street.

"I hope you were thoroughly entertained," Pavlik said.

Dexter Greene pointed at the cigarette in Pavlik's mouth. "Those will land your overweight white ass in there," he said, thumbing back over his right shoulder in the direction of the morgue.

Pavlik looked at his watch. "My ex-wife will land my overweight white ass in there," he said. "Because you don't have the proper instincts yet. Two years with homicide, and you still don't have them."

Greene sat behind the wheel of the Ford Taurus that they were using. He was a short black man with an athletic build. He appeared younger than his thirty-eight years. He was married with three kids.

Pavlik took a long drag on his cigarette once he was inside of the car. Greene immediately opened his window.

"You're just like a woman," Pavlik said.

Greene waited until Pavlik tossed the cigarette out of the car before he started the engine.

"Thank you," Greene said, and immediately pulled away from the curb.

"Well, what they have to say?" Pavlik asked.

"I thought you weren't interested."

"I'm not."

"Well?"

"Well what?" Pavlik said. "We have at least another twenty minutes to spend together, and I'm not in the mood to talk about progressive changes in black cinema again."

Greene smiled. "Which you undoubtedly define as *Blackula* or *Super Fly*," he said.

"Actually, I was thinking *Planet of the Apes*," Pavlik said. "The first one."

"Cracker," Greene said.

Pavlik held up an index finger. "One for me," he said.

Greene shook his head.

After a minute, Pavlik said, "Seriously, what they say in there?"

"Not enough," Greene said. "The coroner did a quick look-see and saw the girl had sex. Probably within twenty-four hours."

"The way she was dressed it was probably more like twenty-four minutes," Pavlik said.

"Except it wasn't rape," Greene said. "At least there were no signs of rape. And the killer was up close. With all three of them, up close. Very close."

Pavlik fumbled a cigarette from his pack. "Which means he knew one of them, wouldn't you think?"

Greene saw the cigarette dangling from Pavlik's mouth. "Yeah, I would think so," he said and then quickly pointed to the cigarette. "Not now."

"Relax, I'm just sucking on it."

Greene turned to Pavlik and smiled.

"Right," Pavlik said as he rolled his eyes.

Greene held up an index finger. "Now we tied," he said. He turned onto Second Avenue and headed south. "What do you make of the other thing, the office?"

"What it was," Pavlik said. "A robbery. Soon as we confirm what Singotti was doing the last few days, we'll have a better idea. We have to figure the girl was working with somebody who got greedy."

"Except it seems too easy," Greene said. "Whoever knocked that office off was looking for something."

"The busted-up desk," Pavlik said.

"The computers were bullshit," Greene said. "They didn't even bother to disguise it, leaving all those screens and keyboards."

Pavlik arched his back in an attempt to stretch it. "Except they did take the laptops."

"Big deal," Greene said. "You could carry those out under your arm. There's something too obvious about this. A robbery seems too easy."

Pavlik was playing with his cigarette. "It usually is," he said.

"Not in a triple homicide," Greene said. "That wasn't panic we saw up there today. That was deliberate shit. That was a fucking execution."

Pavlik nibbled at a sesame seed from a bagel that he had eaten earlier. "We'll see," he said. "Once we get the phone records and the rest of the bullshit, we'll see. Don't be surprised, though, it turns out it was simple shit. Somebody panicked and started shooting. These things turn out to be fuck-ups more often than not."

Greene smiled.

"What?" Pavlik asked.

"I'm thinking mob," Greene said. "Or something more sinister than a fuck-up robbery."

"You watch too many cop shows on television," Pavlik said.

"Only the ones with brothers in them," Greene said.

* * * * *

It took Eddie and Diane Senta most of the rest of the night to fall asleep. Eddie was the first to wake up the next day. He used his cell telephone to call Sarah's apartment and find out what had happened the night before. He hung up when the answering machine clicked on.

"Bullshit," he said aloud.

"How did everything go last night?" Diane asked from under the covers.

"That a serious question, Diane?" Eddie asked.

"I meant you and Tommy," Diane said. "Any trouble?"

"No. But there wasn't any money either. Not what we expected. We came out with computers. Half a dozen laptops and a bunch of PC towers. We didn't take the screens and keyboards. We didn't have the time or the space."

"I called you around two o'clock," Diane said. "You didn't answer."

"I wasn't home yet," Eddie said. "You call from his room?"

"Yes."

"He there?"

"He was in the bathroom."

Eddie felt his face tense with anger. He held up a hand. "No more," he said. "I don't want to talk about it again."

* * * * *

Eddie sat up in bed while Diane put her makeup on. Diane used the remote to turn on the television.

"You need to hear that noise now?" Eddie asked.

"I need to know what the weather will be," Diane said. "And the traffic. I'm going to take the car in. I'm so fucking late as it is."

"Why don't you take the day off?" Eddie said.

"Because I can't," Diane said.

"His plane leave today?"

Diane turned to Eddie. "What?"

Eddie lowered the volume on the television. "I read your e-mail exchange from yesterday," he said. "I guessed your password. It wasn't hard."

"Baby," Diane said, "although I really wish you wouldn't go into my e-mails without my. . . ."

"Right, tough shit," Eddie said. "I know his flight leaves at six. You seeing him off?"

Diane was nervous. "You know his name?"

"Don't worry, Diane. If I wanted to do anything, it would have been done last night. Yeah, I know his name. I won't pursue it beyond that."

Diane dropped her head into her hands.

Eddie turned up the volume on the television again. His eyes opened wide when he saw on the news the neighborhood that he had been in the night before. A news reporter was in midstory when Eddie tuned in.

". . . three people were found murdered in an apartment that doubled as a supply room in this Murray Hill apartment building. The bodies of the owner of the office, his office manager, and another man were found gunned down in cold blood. Police are currently checking with the apartment building management about security cameras in the lobby for possible suspects. The names of the victims are being withheld until all family members have been notified. NBC News has learned . . ."

Eddie turned off the television. He remained motionless on the bed.

Diane began sobbing. "Eddie?" she said. "Eddie?"

CHAPTER 21

ETECTIVE PAVLIK STOPPED AT A BAR ON QUEENS
Boulevard in Sunnyside Gardens. The place was nearly empty except for
a few regulars and the bartender, an Irish woman in her late thirties
with a touch of brogue.

Pavlik sat at the bar and slapped a ten-dollar bill on the bar. "Peter
around?" he asked.

"Peter Phalen?" the bartender asked back.

Pavlik nodded. "Whatever you have on tap," he said.

The bartender poured a pint of Budweiser from the tap. "You're
Phalen's cop friend, aren't you?"

"Right," Pavlik said. He took the pint from the bartender, held it up
in a toast, and took a long drink.

The bartender was looking over Pavlik. "You're the boxer?"

"Was the boxer," he said. "Now I'm a lover. Interested?"

She smiled. "I might be," she said.

Pavlik nodded again. "I won't have kids, and I won't let you put
things inside me," he said. "Just to set the ground rules."

The bartender laughed. "Fair enough," she said.

Pavlik drank some more beer. "What about Phalen?"

"He's due in later."

"I need him to look out for something he might come across the next few weeks. Computers. If he hears anything about hot computers, laptops especially."

"Wouldn't you want to ask him about that stuff yourself?"

Pavlik pointed at the bartender. "I know you're his sister," he said. "I figure you'll pass it along."

"You knew all along, did you?"

"The entire time I was here. The instant I saw you. It's Aelish, right?"

The bartender crossed her arms. "It is in fact," she said. "So, am I that ugly or is Peter the gorgeous type himself?"

Pavlik lit a cigarette. "He's good-looking, don't get me wrong," he said. "But he doesn't have those beautiful Emerald Isle eyes you have there."

"Why, thank you, love."

Pavlik toasted her with his pint. "You, love, are welcome."

He downed the remainder of his pint. Aelish Phalen poured him another.

"Can you tell him Alex was here?" Pavlik asked.

"Sure. Alex the retired boxer, current lover and cop, right?"

"Or your betrothed, if it makes you smile to think that way."

The bartender favored Pavlik with a wink. "You never know what makes a girl happy, love," she said.

Pavlik raised his pint. "Never, ever, ever," he said.

* * * * *

Eddie tried to calm Tommy as they walked the circle at Seaview Park in Canarsie. It was windy in the park. Tommy's windbreaker rippled from sudden gusts. Eddie tried to guide Tommy along the track, but Tommy stopped sporadically and walked in circles on the grass.

"What the fuck am I supposed to do?" Tommy asked. "This is fucking crazy. Nobody counted on this to turn into a massacre. We weren't even there!"

Eddie was trying to steer Tommy back toward the track. "Except we were," he said. "But it doesn't have to be us. It doesn't have to be we, Tommy. They won't know you from a fucking hole in the wall."

Tommy waved one arm behind him as he turned away from the track. "They'll know, they'll know," he said. "They always fuckin' know. They figure this shit out every time."

Eddie stopped following Tommy and frowned. "Think about it first," he said. Tommy stopped to look at Eddie. "Take a moment, calm down, and think," Eddie continued. "There's no way they can figure you in this. There is nothing for them to figure out. We take the computers down to the Fountain Avenue incinerator or toss them in Jamaica Bay and that's the end of it. No evidence, no crime."

Tommy shook his head. "It won't work that way," he said. "Something will go wrong."

"What?" Eddie half yelled. He was frustrated with Tommy. "What will go wrong?"

"The computers, for one thing," Tommy said. He pulled at his mustache. "Jimmy, the driver at the place we stored them, he already took two of them with him this morning to sell. What about that?"

Eddie closed his eyes at the thought of the computers being sold on the street. "Can't you call him back? Beep him or something? Tell him to bring them back."

"I already tried that," Tommy said. "Soon as you called me. I called to make sure everything was still there, and they told me Jimmy took two laptops with him on the truck. The guy's a hustler. He's been taking orders two days already. I told you, he's got some guy in Queens he deals with."

"Fuck," Eddie said. He rubbed at his chin. "Well, that's two laptops in a very big city to track down. If they even bother to look."

"Oh, come on," Tommy said. "It was a triple fuckin' murder. On Park-fuckin'-Avenue, for Christ sakes. They'll look, Eddie. You know they'll look."

Eddie waved at Tommy to walk on the track. "You're getting your sneakers all wet on the grass there," Eddie said.

Tommy looked down at his feet as he headed back toward Eddie. "Fuck my sneakers," he said.

Eddie continued to try to calm Tommy as they walked the half-mile oval. Eddie observed Tommy while he spoke. He took long deliberate drags from a cigarette as he registered Tommy's responses.

"Look," Eddie said. "I need to know you won't break down on me, Tommy. I need to know, no matter what, you'll hold your story." He stopped a moment. "I worked there. I knew the girl. I called the girl. She called me. They may have me. They don't know you." Eddie stopped again. "You don't exist. Nobody knows you from a hole in the wall. I can handle my end. I can deal with whatever happens."

Tommy nervously combed his hair with both hands. "What if they find out?" he asked. "With everything you just said, what if they find out I was with you? What if they know something you don't know they know? If some security camera, like the one the news mentioned at that apartment, caught us on tape somehow. We were right next to a fucking Citibank, Eddie. Maybe you didn't figure on the cameras in the Citibank."

It was a possibility that Eddie was trying to ignore. He frowned at Tommy for bringing it up. "That's a long shot, Tommy. How many long shots you hit in your life?"

"Yeah, exactly," Tommy said. "With my luck, this'll be the fuckin' first."

"I think we have to take that chance," Eddie said.

"But why?" Tommy asked. "We didn't kill those people."

"Because unless we walk in there and confess, they don't have us for anything. Niente'. Nada."

Tommy wasn't convinced. He shook his head. "I got a bad feeling on this, Eddie," he said. "What if we just plea? What if we just tell them, yeah, we robbed the joint and the girl let us in, but that was it, which it was. Why don't we just come clean now so we don't make it any worse than it already is."

"You're not hearing me, Tommy," Eddie said. "Because the least we have to admit to is a felony. That's time. You're shitting your pants at the thought of time right now. We admit anything, we're gone. They can't find the guy who did this, we're gone for life. Or we're dead, because of that law they got now. New York is a death penalty state."

Tommy was flustered. He continued to pull at one end of his mustache. "Maybe we go get ourselves a lawyer and let him do the talking for us," he said.

Eddie stopped walking. "Are you fucking kidding me?" he asked. "A fucking lawyer? A lawyer will have you and me blaming each other in two seconds. They'll both look to cut deals and in the end we'll both do twice the time, or at least one of us will. We might as well confess to the fucking murders we had nothing to do with."

Tommy grabbed at his head in panic. "I don't know, Eddie," he pleaded. "I don't know. If you give them that guy, we should be all right. They should find him."

"What if they don't feel like looking?" Eddie said. "We go in and plea, they have a ready-made guilty party. That fucking neighborhood, Murray Hill, you said it yourself, they'll want blood for this thing. They were rich people got shocked over the weekend. They're not used to that kind of thing, thugs walking in one of their apartments and shooting them. No, Tommy, we can't do a fucking thing until they come to us. And they won't come to you. Not unless we fuck up, which we already did letting that driver take two of those computers. So why don't we concentrate on getting those computers back and making sure we get rid of the rest of them before we fuck ourselves up for real. There's nothing to be gained providing the law with details they may never find out on their own. Let's just take care of our end, and maybe find this piece of shit killed Sarah and those two guys."

Tommy was sweating. "And what if he knew about us, Eddie? What if that broad told him about us?"

Eddie held up a hand. "If he tells them about anybody, Tommy, it won't be you. He doesn't know you. If he tells them anything about any-body, it'll be me. And I'll worry about that bridge when I cross it, okay?"

Tommy was pulling at both ends of his mustache. He shrugged his shoulders unwillingly. Eddie remembered the kid who had lost his father from a sudden heart attack thirty years ago. He remembered how close he and Tommy had become afterward. He reached out to the same kid in an attempt to brace Tommy's life one more time.

"Okay, Tommy?" Eddie asked. "I need to hear you say it's okay."

Tommy stared at Eddie a few seconds. "Okay," he finally said. It was barely a whisper.

CHAPTER 22

DIANE WAS PACKING WHEN EDDIE RETURNED HOME. The scene in their bedroom surprised him. Three half-packed suitcases were opened on their bed. Diane was folding clothes into one of the suitcases when Eddie entered the room. He stopped a few feet inside of the bedroom.

"When the going gets rough, huh?" he said.

Diane folded a sweatshirt. "I figured it had something to do with that report on the television this morning, the way you went pale," she said.

Eddie walked all of the way into the bedroom and lit a cigarette.

"I'm going to stay with a friend," Diane said.

"Excuse me?" Eddie said. "I think we're both passed the bullshit stage here. You're going to California, just say so. Don't sweat it, Di, I won't go looking for the scumbag."

"I'm seeing my therapist," Diane said. "This afternoon. To help me sort this out. I don't know what else to do."

Eddie stepped back. "Your therapist? I hope the fuck you don't intend to tell Esther about. . . ."

"Of course I do," Diane said. "I have to."

"Bull-fucking-shit you have to," Eddie yelled. "Hey, this is serious shit here, Diane. I'm having enough trouble dealing with Tommy right now. I don't need anybody else to worry about."

"It's confidential," Diane said.

"About you!" Eddie yelled. "What about me?"

"It's confidential," Diane repeated.

Eddie bit his lower lip.

"This might be a good time to talk to someone your. . . ."

Eddie waved her off. "Please," he said.

Diane stopped packing to light a cigarette. "If your luck ran out, Eddie, you'd better figure out what you're going to do next. I can't be a part of that. If you had anything to do with. . . ."

"What the fuck is wrong with you?" Eddie asked through clenched teeth. "Of course I didn't have anything to do with that. Jesus Christ, Diane."

Diane attempted to suppress her own rage. "Well, what the hell am I supposed to think, damn you!"

Eddie glared at his wife until she looked away from him.

"You clam up like that and get your stuff and run out of the house and you don't say a fucking word to me," Diane continued. "What the hell am I supposed to think?"

"It's a mess, Diane," Eddie said. "But I didn't kill anybody. Neither did Tommy."

"Then what the fuck happened? Why didn't you say something to me? Why didn't you talk to me?"

"It's just a mess," Eddie said. "There's no point in going into it anymore than to say the woman who brought this thing to me was involved with some black guy, some fucking convict, and he's the one who killed her and her boss and the other guy. She must have arranged for him to steal the guy's gold, that's what her boss was supposed to be buying, Krugerrands or some shit, and she must've told him about me getting the cash, and he went for both the cash and the gold. She never told me she was going after the gold. She wanted revenge against her boss. That's all this was supposed to be for her. She was getting a third of the money. She got a convict involved and I should've known better is the long story short. This guy, the convict, he's the one whacked everybody."

"And now you and Tommy are what? What happens to you two?"

Eddie rubbed his face with both hands. "I have no fucking idea," he said. "Tommy is coming apart at the thought of doing time. At the suggestion that we'd be charged with a murder we didn't commit. Which is why I don't need you running off to your therapist and telling her about it."

Diane shifted her weight to one leg. "Don't tell me you're not worried about being charged, Eddie. Jesus Christ, please don't tell me that. For your son's sake, don't tell me that."

Eddie bit his lower lip again. "What I'm thinking is we shouldn't panic, me and Tommy. They don't have a thing on Tommy. No connection to this thing at all, and me they can only speculate on. I called Sarah. She called me, my cell phone, from the office. I could say I was banging her. I don't have to admit I robbed the office."

Diane cocked her hip. "And you really think they'll believe that, the police?"

"I think it's worth a try," Eddie said.

Diane took a deep breath. "I can't be a part of this," she said.

"Look, I didn't kill anybody, Diane," Eddie said. "That's something they can never pin on me because I didn't do it. The worst that can happen is they nail me for the robbery, which I'm not so anxious to let happen, especially if they don't find the real killer, because then I'll be the scapegoat gets the maximum for some bullshit B and E. They get me for that, I take my lumps. But that doesn't mean I have to feed them this thing. It doesn't mean Tommy and I should go soft at the hint of doing time. Christ, I was Tommy, I'd get some Valium and relax already. I won't give him up. For what? What the fuck could I give him up for?"

"You're convincing yourself, Eddie," Diane said.

"I'm trying to keep my head," Eddie said.

Diane put out her cigarette and continued to pack. "No," she said. "You're convincing yourself."

CHAPTER 23

SINGLETON HAD TAKEN A ROOM IN A MOTEL OFF OF the Saw Mill River Parkway in Westchester. He was waiting for his former cellmate's cousin, the Russian mobster with a crew operating out of Brooklyn. He waited for the Russian across the street from the motel. He waited nearly half-an-hour before a blonde man with a ponytail knocked on the motel room door. When Singleton was comfortable that the Russian was alone, he crossed the street and introduced himself.

"James," Singleton told the Russian man as he extended his right hand. "My friends call me Jimmy."

The Russian was tall and thin and in his early thirties. He wore his dirty-blonde hair in a long ponytail tied with rubber bands. He was wearing a black leather jacket, slacks, and shoes. He surveyed the area before looking down at Singleton's hand and finally accepting it. He didn't say a word.

Singleton opened the motel room door and stepped inside ahead of the Russian. The Russian stopped at the doorway and looked inside before entering.

"You Demi, huh?" Singleton asked.

"Dimi," the Russian said with a heavy accent. His voice was deep and expressionless.

"Huh?" Singleton said. "What, like the actress, right? Demi Moore?" He curved a shapely figure in the air with both his hands. "You know the one I'm talking about?"

"Dimi, no Demi," the Russian said, again without expression. "Don't fock with me."

Singleton held up both his hands. "Dimi, that's what I said. No problem."

The Russian was still standing in front of the door. Singleton motioned to it. "You want to close that?" he asked.

The Russian stepped to one side. Singleton crossed the room and closed the door.

"Vat you vant?" the Russian asked, after the door was closed.

"Victor talked to you, right? About something hot I have you can move for me."

The Russian remained silent.

"My man, you got to show some interest here or I can go talk to a wall," Singleton said. The Russian glared at him. Singleton repeated the question. "Your cousin talked to you, right?"

"Stupid cousin," the Russian said.

"Yeah, well, no argument here about Victor. He should be comin' out soon, though. Yes or no?"

The Russian waved it off. "In, out, alvays same shit."

Singleton smiled. "Which is why I asked him to call you. Your cousin said you out more than in."

"Vat you vant?" the Russian asked again. "I'm busy."

Singleton pulled a Krugerrand from his front pants pocket. "This," he said. He flipped the coin at the Russian.

The Russian caught the coin without effort. He examined it briefly and frowned. "I give you fifty dollar for it," he said. "Not vorth drive from Brooklyn."

Singleton held his smile. "I got more," he said, "lots more."

* * * * *

Singleton explained the deal that he wanted to make to the Russian in the motel parking lot. The Russian was still holding the gold coin in his right hand. Singleton pointed to it.

"The man got the rest of those coins was my partner," Singleton said.

"Vas partner?" the Russian asked.

"Was," Singleton said. "Now he being stingy. Greedy. Cheap. Now he trying to cheat me."

The Russian lit a cigarette. "Make point," he said. "I go see voman after this bullshit."

Singleton smiled again. "Go get yourself some poontang, huh?" he said. "I know what that's about."

The Russian took a deep frustrated breath.

Singleton said, "I'll arrange a meeting with my partner. Tell him I have a buyer for the coins. You show up, take care of business, we make a deal."

The Russian frowned. "Coin is vorth, vat, three-hundred on market?" he asked. "You vant to kill partner, still sell coin? How many coins you have to sell, black man?"

Singleton scratched at the back of his head. "Black man, I like that," he said. "Lots. I have lots of coins to sell."

"Don't fock with me," the Russian said. "How many?"

Singleton dead-eyed the Russian. "Twenty large worth," he said. "But don't get confused about the terms, my friend. My partner isn't worth near that amount. This is no tit-for-tat deal I'm talking about."

The Russian glared into Singleton's eyes. "How much you vant for coins?" he asked.

"What you quoted before," Singleton said. "How's that? Fifty dollars per coin. You take care of business and I make a few bucks. Fair is fair."

The Russian was still glaring. "One more time," he said. "How many coins?"

"Sixty or so," Singleton said. "Something like that. I didn't bother counting. Like I said, my partner has them. Except for that one you holding there, my man."

The Russian took a long drag on his cigarette. He looked down at the coin and slipped it into his front pants pocket. "Business expense," he said.

Singleton smiled as he winked at the Russian. "Minus fifty," he said.

The Russian smirked. "Who is partner?"

Singleton showed his teeth smiling this time. He reached into his back pants pocket and pulled out a piece of paper with an address and telephone number written on it. He handed the paper to the Russian.

"Eddie Senta," Singleton said. "Guy named Eddie Senta."

* * * * *

Dimi handed his cousin, Victor, a twenty-dollar bill in a gas station half a mile from the motel off Saw Mill Parkway. "For gas," Dimi told his cousin.

"What did he say?" Victor asked.

"Bullshit," Dimi said. "But you vatch vat he does anyvay. Just in case."

Victor held up the twenty-dollar bill. "What if I get hungry?" he asked.

"Bite fingernail," Dimi said.

Victor frowned as he watched his cousin pull out of the gas station. He unconsciously chewed at a fingernail on his bandaged hand.

CHAPTER 24

EDDIE PICKED UP TOMMY AND DROVE THE SAAB TO A local Brooklyn car service, where the dispatcher was one of his loan-sharking customers. He parked in the small lot behind the dispatcher's office. He had traded two weeks in payments for the use of a light-blue Dodge Aries that the car service used.

Eddie paged another loan-sharking customer for help. George Waters, a forty-eight-year-old captain in the corrections department at the Riker's Island Penitentiary, owed Eddie more than fifteen hundred dollars from gambling debts. Eddie told the lifelong horseplayer that he would meet him at the finish wire in the Belmont Race Track grandstand.

"I don't think we should be doing this right now," Tommy said. He was consumed with worry.

Eddie offered Tommy a cigarette. Tommy shook off the offer.

"You look sick," Eddie said.

"I feel sick," Tommy said.

"We need to get back to a routine," Eddie said. "You do. We both do. We can't sit around watching the television. You can't worry about things out of your control, Tommy. We need to move on. I'm going back to work with the computers first job I can get."

"And what if they find us here?" Tommy said. "At the track, for Christ sakes. Collecting shy money, no less."

Eddie pulled up to the parking gate and handed the woman working the booth a five-dollar bill. She handed Eddie three dollars back, which Eddie stashed in the sun visor.

"You're starting to sound as sick as you look," Eddie told Tommy. "How the hell are they going to know about shy money? You're coming apart."

* * * * *

After Eddie paid their admission into the track, Tommy followed him through the building to the grandstand. There was a smaller-than-usual crowd. Eddie noticed there were still eight minutes to post time before the next race. He looked for George Waters in the crowd near the finish line. He spotted the big man at one of the concession stands.

Waters was a heavyset black man. He wore thick glasses and walked with a limp from an injury incurred on the job during a prison riot. He was staring at the tote board near the finish line as he ate a frankfurter when Eddie approached him. His racing program was folded under one arm.

"You doing anything?" Eddie asked.

"Losing," Waters said. He spoke in an emotionless, even monotone. "Steady, too. Ten bucks a race for six races. What's so important, you come to this place?"

Eddie put a hand on Tommy's shoulder. "This is a good friend of mine," he told Waters. "Tommy G."

Waters shook Tommy's hand and nodded. "George," Waters said.

"Nice to meet you," Tommy said.

Waters turned to Eddie. "I saw that movie," he said. "Friend of mine, friend of ours."

Eddie rolled his eyes. "You watch too many movies," he said.

"How do you handle it in there?" Tommy asked Waters. "In a prison, I mean. Day after day."

"And night after night," Waters said. He shrugged. "Same as you handle your twenty-four/seven. That's all it is, time. In or out, we all make our own twenty-four hours fit. Every day, seven days a week. You inside, you outside, you still doing time."

"George is a part-time philosopher," Eddie said.

"What I am is a fool trying to figure these animals out," he said. "I play the chalk and get burned by the long shots. I play the long shots, they trip coming out the gate. It's a lose-lose proposition."

"I need a favor," Eddie said.

"That's a change," Waters said. "What can I do for you?"

"I need you to look for somebody inside the joint," Eddie said. "A guy was released a few weeks ago, maybe a month. Maybe more."

Waters bit into his frankfurter as he looked from Eddie to Tommy. "That narrows it down," he said. "What, he got a line of you guys forming for him?"

"Something like that," Eddie said.

Waters glanced up at the odds board. "I hope you got more than what you told me, a black guy let out the last few months."

Eddie wrote the name on the racing program. "James," he said. "That's his name. Maybe. If he wasn't bullshitting somebody. Except he was in for robbery. At least I think he was."

Waters finished the last of his frankfurter and wiped his mouth with the napkin that he was holding. "And he was upstate?"

Eddie looked confused. "I assume so," he said. "I'm not sure."

Waters read the name off the program. "You full of information on this boy, huh?"

"Can you do anything for me?" Eddie asked.

Waters nodded again. "Now that I'm administration, I can," he said. "If the boy was a robber. If the boy's name is James. If he was released the last month or so. That's your best chance, the release date and his name."

"It's worth five hundred, George," Eddie said.

Waters eyes opened wide. "Boy must owe big."

"Can you do it?"

Waters nodded one more time. "I'm leaving after the next race," he said. "I'll call you as soon as I have something."

Eddie pulled four fifty-dollar bills from his wallet and slapped it in George's right hand. "I appreciate it," Eddie said.

Waters' eyes opened wide again. "Damn," he said. "I'm glad I'm not this boy you looking for."

"You got that right," Eddie said.

＊ ＊ ＊ ＊ ＊

Back in the parking lot, Tommy was uncomfortable again. He pulled at one end of his mustache. "I don't know I like it your friend equating everything to doing time," Tommy said.

Eddie forced a smile. "George is just rationalizing," he said. "You should've done your Mick Jagger for him. Time is on your side or something."

"I'm not feeling funny, Eddie."

"You're slipping, Tommy. It isn't that bad yet. You have to relax. Your mind is working overtime on this."

"What about Joe Sharp?" Tommy asked. "Why don't you go to him with this, see what he says. He always looks after you."

Eddie took a deep breath. "Look, Tommy, I already asked two different people for favors today, and I may have to ask somebody else for another one down the road. That's not my style. I don't like to reach out if I don't have to. The more you ask for favors, the more complicated your life becomes. Especially in our world.

"Joe Sharp, no matter how much he might like me, is a high-profile wiseguy. That means he's a target of surveillance he can never truly beat, not in the long run. It's why none of the wiseguys want to be boss anymore. It's why the guys with the options don't want to be made.

"So, no, we shouldn't bring this to Joe Sharp. I shouldn't. Neither should you. Joe Sharp has enough problems without the attention a triple homicide brings. Right now there's no reason to do anything. We're fine we stay in the shadows we know. We reach out for the wrong reasons, things get fucked up and complicated. If you let yourself breathe again, you'll see we're fine."

"Except you're looking for the black dude now," Tommy said. "The one you think killed those people."

"That's right," Eddie said. "Just in case. To feed the cops if we have to. If we have to."

Tommy pulled hard on one end of his mustache. "Just in case?" he said. "Somehow that doesn't make me breathe any easier, Eddie. It doesn't make me comfortable at all."

CHAPTER 25

DIANE LOOKED OUT OF THE EIGHTH-FLOOR WINDOW OF her therapist's office onto Washington Square Park. It was still a sunny day. The park was crowded. People seemed to be gathering near a portable bandstand. Diane took a deep breath as the office door opened across the room.

"Your feeling guilty is a natural response," Esther Lincoln said.

She was an attractive, middle-aged woman dressed in a yellow-and-white sundress. She had colored red hair and light blue eyes. A single strand of pearls hung from her neck. She had just come into her office from the reception area. She carried a fresh pitcher of water and set it on a tray on the edge of her desk.

They had just finished the first half-hour of their session. Diane had already told her therapist about what had happened to Eddie and about her affair with her boss. She sat in the chair in front of the black wood desk and played with a tissue in her right hand.

"My feeling stupid isn't normal, though," Diane said. "I don't usually feel stupid about what I do."

Esther poured herself a glass of water. "Because of Eddie?" she asked.

"Because of me," Diane said. "Mike, my boss. Because of going through with that."

"That was one of the risks," Esther said. "You knew that going in. Even if you had planned to try, there was never a guarantee you'd get pregnant the first time. You might have to try again and again."

"Yes, well, there was another way to handle that," Diane said.

Esther sipped her water. "Except you knew that part of the experience involved sleeping with Mike. Because Eddie wasn't interested in more children of his own."

Diane rubbed her forehead.

"I don't see where you did wrong," Esther said. "You were honest with Eddie, both before and after. You did warn him, didn't you? That's what you said on the telephone."

"I did wrong to myself," Diane said. "Going to bed with Mike. That was wrong. For me, it was wrong."

Esther waited for more. When Diane started to sob, Esther said, "Again, these feelings are quite normal. You shouldn't beat yourself up over them. What's done is done."

"I don't know that I want to be patted on the back right now," Diane said. "I made a mistake. I know it was a mistake. I shouldn't have done this. Eddie was right. I was wrong."

"You're feeling sorry about Eddie is also quite normal," Esther said.

Diane slapped her knees. "Why the fuck can't you blame me for this?" she snapped. "It was wrong, damn it! I was wrong. Eddie was right."

Esther sipped more water. "Because this is your therapy, not Eddie's," she finally said. "This isn't about being right or wrong."

Diane rolled her eyes. "Jesus Christ," she said.

"You need to get over the guilt," Esther continued. "You're entitled to want things. Especially a child. You shouldn't feel guilty about wanting anything in this life, Diane."

"Right, because this is my therapy," Diane said in a mocking tone. "Would Eddie's therapist give him the same advice for not wanting a baby?"

Esther didn't respond.

"I need to be there for him now," Diane said. "Especially after what's happened to him."

"That isn't something you can control," Esther said.

"He's my husband."

"He's also an adult. That was his choice. You made it clear beforehand that you wanted nothing to do with what he was involved in. You've been telling him that all along. His life, that life, scares most people. From what you've told me, you've made that very clear to Eddie."

Diane shook her head. "It isn't that black and white," she said. "How the hell can you expect me to deal with it that way? Christ, Esther, show some feeling. You're so fucking cold sometimes."

"Because you're here for you, not Eddie," Esther said. "No matter how hard it is for you to hear that. No matter how cold it sounds coming from me."

Diane threw her hands up. "This is bullshit," she said. "This is just bullshit."

"Now you sound like Eddie."

"Now I'm making sense."

"No, you're still feeling guilty. For something you didn't have any control over. For something out of your realm of responsibility."

"Christ, in that case, let me sell the house from under his feet. Let me empty the bank accounts and make a run for it."

"To California?"

"I don't think so."

A long pause followed. Esther didn't flinch.

"I suppose it would be all right if I did go, though, wouldn't it?" Diane asked in a mocking tone again.

Esther slowly frowned. "If that's what you really wanted," she said. "I don't think running away from his life would be the wrong thing to do. It might be dangerous to stay there."

Diane's hands had balled into fists. "It's not right," she said. "It's just not right for me."

"That's my point," Esther said. "What you did with your boss was your decision. That was your responsibility. Even Eddie recognized that. What Eddie did was his decision. You shouldn't feel guilty over it."

"And he didn't throw me out of the house when I told him, either," Diane said.

"Maybe he's more in love with you than you are with him. Maybe the reality of Mike jolted him. Maybe he's starting to realize what he's losing. Or maybe he's got more urgent issues on his mind. What you've told me today certainly qualifies."

"And maybe he was just doing the right thing. But it seems you don't want to give him credit for that."

"I'm just pointing out the fact that Eddie did what Eddie wanted. For Eddie's sake, not yours."

Diane moved up on her chair. "And maybe I need to help him now. Maybe that's the right thing to do for me."

"It is a maternal instinct, to protect."

"Is that a cheap shot, or are you pointing out something else for me?"

"I'm offering you options."

Diane stood up from her chair. "Yeah, well, I don't want any right now," she said. "I think what I'll do is just go ahead and follow my instincts this time. No grand plans. No big conversations about what I want. I think I'll just go and be there for Eddie and see where that takes me."

Esther glanced at her watch. "That may work," she said. "We still have some time left."

"I'm in a kind of a rush," Diane said with sarcasm.

"Maybe you want to think about it," Esther said. "I can step outside for a few minutes. We still have another fifteen minutes."

"Don't bother," Diane said. "I'm going home to Eddie. I think he can use my help right now. He needs my support. And at least I'll know I did the right fucking thing. At least I'll know that."

CHAPTER 26

EDDIE STOOD IN THE FRONT PARLOR OF HIS HOUSE watching the street. He watched a squirrel gathering chestnuts in a neighbor's yard. He watched the squirrel scurry down the tree, gather a chestnut, and return in quick uniform movements.

When the squirrel finally disappeared from Eddie's view, he sat down in a chair in the living room and set an ashtray on his right leg. He crushed out the remainder of a cigarette in the ashtray until the ash turned to a fine gray dust. He remembered watching his father do the same thing. Whenever Eddie Sr. was deep in thought, he would crush a cigarette in an ashtray over and over until life snapped him out of whatever had put him in a trance-like state.

Fewer than twelve months earlier, Eddie had watched his father crush out one of his last cigarettes. Eddie had brought his father to a Stamford, Connecticut hospital shortly after Eddie Sr. was in a car accident. The old man had hurt his back and was waiting for X ray results in an emergency room bed. He had started a coughing fit that lasted more than five minutes before the old man could stop himself.

Eddie had told his father, "While you're in here, why don't you get that checked out?"

Eddie Sr. had waved his son off. "And why don't you go get me a *Playboy* or something?" he had said. "A man visits another man in the hospital, he brings him a dirty magazine. Don't you know that?"

"I'm the one brought you here," Eddie said. "I'm not visiting."

"Whatever," the old man said. "Don't you remember when you were in the hospital with that sickness thing you had from eating the seafood? The salmonella thing? I brought you a *Playboy*."

"Uncle Frank brought me the *Hustler*," Eddie said. "*Hustler* showed snatch."

"Uncle Frank was always a bigger pervert 'n me," Eddie Sr. said.

Eddie smiled. "I caught Jack with a *Hustler* not too long ago," he told his father.

The old man smiled. "Was he beating his pud?"

Eddie laughed. "I guess so. I saw it under his bed when I was setting up his bookshelves. I didn't say anything."

The old man nodded. "Speaking of your son, I think it's time you start thinking of him and letting this other shit you do go. Before it's too late."

Eddie had just nodded at his father.

"Its one of the things I regret most," Eddie Sr. said. "Showing you that world. Letting you get worked up over it. You thought it was something dramatic. You looked up to it. I wish I'd never let you even see it."

"You don't have to worry about Jack," Eddie told his father. "He's a lot smarter than I am. A lot."

"He's got your temper," the old man said.

"He's just as messy as I was when I was a kid," Eddie said. "And he loves sports more than anything. But he's smarter. He's got it all over me. Not even close. He'll be fine. He won't go anywhere near this bullshit I do. Don't worry about it."

Eddie Sr. had nodded again. "I hope not," he said.

A short time later, an emergency room doctor introduced one of the resident doctors at the hospital to Eddie and his father. The resident explained how they found a large black spot in the area of the old man's chest in the back X ray. There was a good chance, since Eddie Sr. was a smoker, that the black spot might be cancerous. They asked for permission to perform an immediate biopsy. A few days later, Eddie Sr. was diagnosed with terminal lung cancer. Four months later, he was dead from the disease.

The sound of the telephone ringing broke Eddie's concentration. He let go of the cigarette butt he was still crushing ashes with and headed for the kitchen. When he answered the phone, he immediately heard a click as the line went dead.

CHAPTER 27

THE APARTMENT BUILDING WHERE LARRY SINGOTTI had lived was a lush condominium in Murray Hill, not far from his office. The four-bedroom apartment was valued at more than three million dollars. As they stood in the marble pantry, Detectives Greene and Pavlik watched Melanie Singotti directing the mourner traffic inside of the apartment. She was wearing a black turtleneck blouse, a black leather skirt, black nylons, and black high heels. Both detectives noticed that she had removed her wedding ring.

"She doesn't look very happy," Pavlik whispered to Greene.

"Duh," Greene whispered back. "Her husband was murdered."

"No, I mean she don't look very upset."

"She's not. He was with another broad."

Pavlik bumped his head against Greene's head. "You know what the fuck I mean," he said.

Greene rubbed the left side of his head as Mrs. Singotti approached them. "Can I help you?" she asked.

They had already been introduced. Pavlik reminded the widow why they were there. "About Mr. Singotti, ma'am."

Greene added: "And the other woman."

Mrs. Singotti smiled at both detectives. "Yes," she said. "The little lush-slash-slut, his office manager, Sarah. I knew all about them. Going back more than four years. What else?"

Pavlik looked to Greene before asking Mrs. Singotti. "To be fair, ma'am, there was another man with Mr. Singotti. And. . . ."

Mrs. Singotti interrupted Pavlik. "You can tell that to the daughters, detective. The girls will need something to console them. I'm an adult. I know better. Anything else?"

Greene referred to his notes. "Your husband went to the bank the day he was murdered," he said. "He visited a safe deposit box. Do you know anything about that box? What might've been inside?"

Mrs. Singotti bit her lower lip. "Visited?" she asked. "No, I don't know anything about that particular safe deposit box, and, as you might imagine, I'm very anxious to learn more about it. As for why he went to visit it, well, I would assume to withdraw or deposit something. Something I would never know about. No doubt he shared the box with his grieving daughters, right? I'm sure both their names are shown as co-signers on the box."

Pavlik nodded. "Yes, ma'am," he said.

Mrs. Singotti took a deep breath. "Anything else, gentlemen?"

Greene closed his notebook. "Did your husband mention anything that might suggest a problem?"

"Was he a gambler, ma'am?" Pavlik asked.

"Did he bet with bookmakers?" Greene added.

Mrs. Singotti laughed. "As in the mob?" she asked. "Please. Larry would soil himself watching *Goodfellas* on the VCR. No, he wasn't a gambler. He may have had enemies in the business he was in, but he never mentioned them to me. Listen, detectives, if you don't already know this you will soon enough. Larry was a cheap fuck is what he was."

Pavlik nodded again. "I see," he said.

"Anything else?" Mrs. Singotti asked one more time.

"No ma'am," Greene said.

"No ma'am," Pavlik said.

Mrs. Singotti smiled, nodded, and returned to the mourners in her living room. Greene went up on his toes to whisper in Pavlik's right ear. "All righty then," he said.

* * * * *

The detectives made a series of phone calls using their cell phones from the street before they stopped for lunch. They were eating pizza on the corner of Twenty-ninth Street and Third Avenue as they compared notes. Pavlik turned off his cell phone and grabbed a hot slice from the counter. He stepped back as he bit into the slice. Greene picked at the cheese on his slice with a fork.

"Strike gold?" Greene asked.

Pavlik chewed on his pizza as he held the folded slice over a napkin. He let the grease drip off the end onto the napkin. The napkin was soon spotted with a reddish-gold color.

"The computers," Pavlik said. "Maybe. I have to see a guy later about them. Some guy in Queens. What about you?"

"The phone calls lead to a guy named Eddie Senta," Greene said. He sipped at a can of Diet Coke. "At least that's who's paying the cell phone bills."

"Isn't that the guy we found on the office payroll thing?" Pavlik asked. He held the slice of pizza away from his body again as he took another bite.

"He worked as a temp at Singotti's office," Greene said. "About six or seven months ago. Word processor. Worked there two weeks, and that was that."

"Triple-murder-killer-and-thief word processor?"

"Or a faggot," Greene said as he chewed on hot cheese. "My wife used to do that work before the kids. She said most of the men word processors she knew were gay. Of course, that was twelve, thirteen years ago."

"We'll find out soon enough," Pavlik said before taking another small bite.

"I have calls down to St. Thomas about our friend Ivan," Greene said. "See maybe our brethren down there can tell us something."

"'Brethren' . . . I like that," Pavlik said.

"It's practice," Greene said. "It's what we gonna call each other instead of brother once the great revolution comes."

Pavlik belched. "Great revolution this," he said.

"I'm also gonna run our friend, Eddie Senta, through O.C.," Greene said.

Pavlik was drinking from his can of soda. "Huh?" he said. "The faggot word processor?"

"We don't know he's a faggot yet," Greene said. "He could have been doing the wild thing with our lady friend, Ms. Sarah Parker."

"She was a healthy enough girl," Pavlik said.

"She was more than healthy. She was sexually active less than twenty-four hours before the bell tolled."

"Which is another thing you need to check on," Pavlik said. He belched a second time. "Your friends at the morgue."

Greene wiped his mouth with a napkin. "My friends?"

Pavlik winked. "Morgue boys are your brethren, brother."

* * * * *

A few hours later, both detectives met with the owner of the Irish bar that Pavlik had previously visited in his search for the missing computers.

"The guy's out front," Peter Phalen said with a thick Irish accent. He was a tall, broad-shouldered man with curly blonde hair and blue eyes. He wore a loose-fitting plaid shirt and dungarees.

"How'd you get him here?" Greene asked.

They were in the small back office. They had parked around the corner and entered through the back door. It had just turned dark outside.

"Incentive," Phalen said. "The man thinks he has a fish on the line."

"He have a computer with him?" Pavlik asked.

"Not that I know of," Phalen said. "Maybe in his truck. I didn't ask."

Pavlik nudged Phalen. "Your sister here?"

Greene was confused. Phalen rolled his eyes. "He's got it for my sister," he told Greene.

"And she's got it for me," Pavlik said.

"Blind girl?" Greene said. "That's too bad."

Phalen laughed. "Just ignorant," he said. "You know the type. Off the boat and all."

* * * * *

A short heavy man wearing a Yankees baseball cap stood at the bar drinking beer from a bottle. Aelish Phalen smiled at Detective Pavlik as he approached the short man. Peter Phalen went behind the bar to relieve his sister.

Detective Greene flashed his badge at the short man.

"What's this about?" the short man asked.

"A triple murder," Pavlik said.

"What?" the short man said.

"Where'd you get the computers you were selling?" Greene asked.

The short man feigned confusion. "What computers?"

Peter Phalen winked at the short man. "Don't bother," he said. "They already know about the computers."

The short man took a moment. "I didn't take them," he said.

"Who did?" Pavlik asked.

"I don't know."

"Did we mention the triple murder thing?" Greene asked Pavlik.

"I think so," Pavlik said. He turned to the short man. "I mentioned that, right, the people killed who worked at the office where the computers were stolen?"

"What people?" the short man asked as he stepped back. "What the fuck is going on here?" He looked to Phalen. "What's up with this?"

Phalen motioned toward Pavlik with his head. "Tell the man what he wants to know," he said.

"We're waiting," Greene said.

The short man shook his head nervously. "I got them at work," he said. "Some guy dumped them off, and I grabbed two. I didn't know him. I never seen the guy before."

Greene cracked his knuckles. "One more time, then we take you in," he said.

"What for?" the short man asked. "I didn't do nothin'."

"You read the papers?" Greene asked the short man.

"You read?" Pavlik followed up with.

"What?" the short man asked. "What's this about?"

"Last time," Greene said. "A triple murder."

"The computers were stolen from an office," Pavlik said. "The guy owned the business was killed a couple blocks away. Him and two other people. One and two makes three. Thus, a triple murder."

The short man's eyes opened wide. "That thing on the news? Holy shit!"

"Right," Greene said. He patted the short man on the right arm.

The short man raised both his hands. "Hey, that wasn't me, pal. No way. I'm no killer."

"The computers," Pavlik said. He leaned toward the short man with a hard stare.

The short man stuttered. "Huh? Ah, ah, oh, that," he said. His eyes opened wide a second time. "You're saying those are the computers?"

Greene smiled at Pavlik. "He catches on quick," Greene said.

"Oh, shit," the short man said. "Tommy. Tommy Gaetani brought those in. Guy named Tommy Gaetani."

Greene held his smile. "See?" he said to Pavlik. "All we had to was ask."

CHAPTER 28

OMMY HAD TROUBLE SLEEPING THE NIGHT BEFORE. He had tried Valium, scotch, and NyQuil cold and flu medicine, but his nerves wouldn't allow him to rest. Shortly after noon, after starting and stopping himself from calling Eddie to tell him that he couldn't stand waiting to be arrested and that he wanted to go to the police, the police called Tommy at his house. Tommy's wife answered. She told the police that Tommy wasn't home yet. She told them that she would have him call them as soon as he walked in. When she hung up, Tommy made a decision to talk to somebody that he thought could help Eddie and him.

Tommy went to Joe Sharpetti's social club on Coney Island Avenue in Brooklyn and told the gangster the entire story. A beefy man stood guard at the back office door.

"Does Eddie know you're here?" Sharpetti asked when Tommy was finished telling the story.

Tommy pulled at his mustache. "No, sir," he said, as he shook his head. "No. I started to call him a few times before I came here, but I couldn't make the call. He doesn't want to hear this from me. He wants me to hold out. And I was holding out until the cops called. I don't see how we hold out anymore. That's why I came to you. He'll listen to you."

"Yous did this job together, you should come to me together," Sharpetti said. "It's not fair to Eddie you're here without him."

Tommy held up both of his hands. "I'm just saying we should take the rap for what it is," he said. "Robbery, Mr. Sharpetti. I'm not trying to make Eddie look bad in your eyes. Please don't think that. Eddie's been nothing but good to me. Ever since I know him."

"Eddie's a good man," Sharpetti said.

"But he thinks we can beat this thing, and I know we can't," Tommy said. "Now the police called my house, so I know it's over. I say we just take the rap for what it is and live with it. Before they try and nail us for a murder we had nothing to do with."

"And what if they followed you here?" Sharpetti asked. "Did you make sure they didn't?"

Tommy's hands went up in the air again. "Yes, sir," he said. "I would never bring the cops here. I checked."

Sharpetti focused on Tommy's eyes. "All right," he said. "Why don't you wait outside a few minutes and let me think what to do. Give me ten minutes. All right?"

Tommy licked his lips. "Sure, Mr. Sharpetti," he said. "I'm sorry to bother you with this, but I know how much you like Eddie. He didn't want me to come to you. Because of the past, the betting and all, but I know you're close with him. I know you can talk to him. I appreciate it you're seeing me. Really."

Sharpetti stood up. Tommy walked around the desk, took Sharpetti's right hand in his, and kissed the old man's cheek.

"Just wait outside a few minutes, and I'll be right with you," the old man said.

* * * * *

The beefy man sat across from Sharpetti once Tommy was out of the office.

"What do you wanna do?" he asked his boss.

Sharpetti lit a short thick cigar. "Lose him," he said.

The beefy man thumbed over his right shoulder. "This guy here, lose?"

Sharpetti pointed toward the door. "He's falling to pieces," he said. "I'll straighten it out with Eddie. He's not going to like it, but this guy has to go."

"Now, tonight?" the beefy man asked.

"What am I speaking fuckin' Greek?" Sharpetti asked.

"I got it," the beefy man said.

Sharpetti waited a moment and then pointed a finger at the beefy man. "And make sure he stays lost," he said. "No fuck-ups."

"Right," the beefy man said.

Sharpetti took a long drag on his cigar and motioned toward the door. "Get going," he said. "Before he soils his pants out there."

* * * * *

Eddie had decided to resume as normal a routine as possible. He called one of the clients he worked with on a request basis and asked if they had work. The midnight supervisor at the law firm that Eddie called was an old friend in the word processing field. Phil Marks had worked with Eddie at a few of the financial firms during the mega-merger days in the 1980s. Marks told Eddie that he could use him for the third shift. Marks then called one of the temporary agencies that Eddie worked through and requested Eddie.

"I appreciate the work," Eddie told Phil Marks when he arrived at the firm.

Marks was sitting behind a long desk facing a sea of cubicles. He was a short fat man. He had lost most of his hair. He was a year younger than Eddie, but the two men shared similar backgrounds. Both had learned a skill to change their work from blue collar to white collar. Both had hustled as temporary operators for many years. Both had been married and divorced. Both had kids.

It was a few minutes after midnight when Marks brought Eddie into the manager's office for a cup of coffee.

"What's with the sudden urge to work again?" Marks asked.

"Marital problems," Eddie said.

"Sorry to hear that. Serious?"

Eddie shrugged one shoulder. "She left me."

"It's been a while since you were here," Marks said. "We added two operators and another proofreader. Things have been busy, but I figured you'd call when you wanted the work. I can put you on pretty steady if you want it."

"At least for now, yeah," Eddie said. "I appreciate it."

"You look tired," Marks said. "You gonna be all right?"

"I'll make it," Eddie said.

"Just let me know if you need a break. That fucking broad is still looking to sink my ship."

"The Asian broad? The pet detective?" Eddie asked.

Marks smirked as he shook his head. "She's started more trouble in this place than you can imagine. She wants to be the big boss someday. The only thing saves my ass in here is the manager couldn't be more comatose. You bring her a problem, she looks the other way. Management by denial. The operations people in this place ever drink coffee without the Valium, the manager's back at a reception desk where she belongs. In the meantime, this other broad, the animal crusader, she's after my ass. Thirty-six years old, not a bad looker for a noodle, but she has nothing better to do than stir the shit."

"Some people can't stop themselves from fucking up a good thing," Eddie said.

"Just don't let her see you nodding off," Marks said. "She'll report you and me. She's done it already. I have two good temps I can't use anymore because of that cunt."

Eddie was confused. "Why don't you fire her?"

Marks jerked the air with a fist. "Like I said, the manager has a fear of making decisions. 'Specially ones she has to answer for."

"Oh, well," Eddie said.

"Exactly," Marks said. "So just let me know if you're starting to go. I'll send you out for fresh air or something."

"Right," Eddie said.

He took a document from the OUT bin and logged onto a workstation in the back of the center. He set up his portable CD player to listen to the radio for news on the murders. The only lead that the radio mentioned was a surveillance camera at the building where Singotti's office storage room was located, where the murders had occurred.

Eddie whispered to himself, "Finally," when he heard mention of the surveillance tape.

Eddie opened the document that he was working on and saw that it involved a merger for a market research firm. He immediately thought of Diane and her boss. He found it hard to concentrate on his work.

He had a hard time staying awake. He forced himself to drink several cups of black coffee to fight his drowsiness. He had slept fewer than twelve hours in three days. Sitting in a word processing center and trying to focus on a computer screen and the small print of the document he was working on, Eddie started to feel the inevitable exhaustion. He took a few walks outside for breaks to wake up. He splashed water on his face at every trip to the men's room. He popped a No-Doz tablet when he thought he was going to crash. When it was finally time to leave, Eddie was relieved.

* * * * *

When he was out on the street, Eddie noticed two men standing near his Saab on Liberty Street. A tall broad man and a shorter black man were huddled together sipping coffee from containers. When Eddie saw that the men were watching him, he knew they were cops. He stopped at a coffee wagon to buy himself a cup of coffee for the ride home. When he left the coffee wagon, both men approached him before he could reach his car. They each flashed detective badges as they introduced themselves.

"I just worked all night, fellas," Eddie told the detectives.

"So did we," the black detective said.

CHAPTER 29

THE DETECTIVES QUESTIONED EDDIE AT THE Elizabeth Street precinct in Chinatown. They used an investigation room with a table and three folding chairs. Detective Greene offered Eddie a cup of coffee. It was clear to Eddie that Greene would be the good cop in whatever routine they had planned. Detective Pavlik remained quiet during the first round of questioning, but his eyes were always focused on Eddie.

After explaining away the exchange of telephone calls with Sarah Parker, Eddie realized that the second round of questions would be issued with a more skeptical attitude. Greene restarted the series of questions, beginning with the telephone calls.

"So, you're telling us that these calls are about therapy?" Detective Greene asked Eddie.

"I told you, we were friends," Eddie said. "Sarah was confused. She's had bad luck with men all her life. She wanted my opinion on this new guy."

"The black guy," Greene said.

"The black guy," Eddie said.

"Was she confused a few hours before she died?" Pavlik suddenly asked.

Eddie was in the middle of a yawn. "Huh?" he said.

"Because you guys spoke to each other, according to two sets of telephone records, not too long before she was killed," Pavlik said. When Eddie seemed puzzled, Pavlik repeated his original question. "Was she confused a few hours before she was murdered?"

Eddie slowly shook his head. "I guess so," he said.

Greene scribbled in a notepad. "That's another thing," he said. "You never called again after those last phone calls. Except for a brief hang-up from your cellular telephone. I guess when the machine clicked on?"

"I didn't want to disturb her," Eddie said.

"Right," Greene said. "But you never called again after that. Not Sarah or her office. Or us for that matter."

"After the murder was all over the papers and television," Pavlik said. "You had to recognize the building location, even if you didn't listen to the details."

"I didn't know about it for, what, two days now?" Eddie said. "I didn't call Sarah again because I just assumed everything had worked itself out. I have my own problems at home. Me and my wife."

"I'm sorry to hear that," Greene said.

"You bangin' this broad or not?" Pavlik asked.

Eddie spoke directly to Greene. "We were involved once," he lied. "After we first met. Six months ago." He held up a finger for emphasis. "Just once."

"Save it for your wife," Pavlik said.

"I hope that doesn't have to become public knowledge," Eddie said. "For my wife's sake."

Pavlik forced a smile. "We'll have to wait and see what else becomes public knowledge first," he said.

Greene glanced at his notes. "How long you been with Joe Sharp's crew?" he asked.

"I'm not with anybody's crew," Eddie said. "You saw the building I came out of. I'm a word processor."

"You know Joe Sharp?" Greene asked, ignoring Eddie's response.

"I know him, yes," Eddie said. "I know Mr. Sharpetti. I met him ten years ago at a Little League parade."

"Right," Greene said. "And the two assault charges from five years ago?"

"Both dismissed," Eddie said. "Street fights. Nothing more dramatic than that. About a parking spot, I think one of them was. The other was on the subway."

"Right," Greene said. "And the fact you're on six separate surveillance tapes at Joe Sharpetti functions, his crew in full mob regalia?"

Eddie spoke to Pavlik this time. "I've been to weddings and baptisms and two funerals where Mr. Sharpetti was also invited or where he was paying his respects." He turned toward Greene. "It's probably just coincidence."

"Right," Greene said. "And the Brooklyn organized crime unit created a folder for you," he said. "Five years ago."

"Anything in it?" Eddie asked.

Pavlik moved a folding chair directly in front of Eddie's chair and sat in it. "You want that kind of heat, asshole, all it would take is a phone call," he said. "You're too small to put under surveillance yet, but you were big enough to get a mention. That's how organized crime units work, numb-nuts. We want to flush you out, consider yourself flushed."

"At a 1991 super bowl party at Bella Bambina's, a lone gunman later identified as an associate with a rival crew with the Vignieri family fired three shots inside the club," Greene said.

"At a table where you were sitting with Joe Sharpetti and two soldiers directly under him," Pavlik added.

"Word is you stood in the path of the bullets," Greene said.

"Between Sharpetti and the gunman," Pavlik said.

"It's a nice fantasy," Eddie said. "I was there at a friend's bachelor party. I was coming out of the bathroom when the guy started shooting. I surprised him. He turned the gun on me."

"Instead of shooting who he was there to shoot?" Pavlik asked.

Eddie looked at Greene. "I'm not a gangster," he said. He turned to Pavlik. "I'm a word processor."

* * * * *

At the point when Eddie could barely stay awake, Detective Greene sat across from him with a cup of coffee. They had been at it for more than two hours. Eddie's voice was dry from lack of sleep.

"One last round of questions," Greene said. "Regarding your story about this black man Sarah had mentioned."

"The convict you didn't bother to find out his name you were so concerned," Pavlik said.

Eddie yawned. "James," he said. "That's his name. James. I don't know his last name. He did time for some kind of robbery, and he was a drinker," Eddie said in a programmed monotone. "That's what Sarah said. That's why I was originally concerned, because of the drinking more than the other thing. Sarah is a recovering alcoholic."

"Yeah, yeah, we know," Pavlik said. "So the guy's name is James. A black man named James."

Eddie nodded.

"But you never saw him, right?" Greene asked.

Eddie shook his head. "Just from the back," he said. "When they came out of the bar a little after midnight."

"And you were in the neighborhood at that time, why?" Pavlik asked.

"I was visiting Sarah," Eddie said. "I was about to. When I saw her with the black guy, I just drove home. She lives up in the nineties, near enough to where I can get the Triborough to the Grand Central."

Pavlik smirked. "A midnight visit? You live on Long Island. That's a long way to drive at that time of night."

"Couldn't you just call her first?" Greene asked.

"I was at a card game," Eddie said. "After the bar. P.G. Kings on Thirty-third Street. A friend of mine owns the restaurant. We had a few drinks there and went around the corner to his apartment for a continental game. We play every couple weeks. That's at least three times I've told you that now."

Greene wrote in his notepad. "There a chance this black guy you say was Sarah's new boyfriend, he knows you?"

"Huh?" Eddie said.

Greene repeated his question. "There a chance Sarah's boyfriend knows you?"

Eddie yawned. "I wouldn't know," he said.

"Only because you might be a loose end," Greene suggested. "If he did the killings."

"If he knows you," Pavlik added.

Eddie shrugged. "I have no idea," he said. "Can I leave now? I'm exhausted."

"In a minute," Greene said. He checked his notepad one more time. "What about Tommy Gaetani?" he asked.

Eddie's head jerked from the question. It was the first time that the detectives had mentioned Tommy. "Ah-what?" he said.

"Tommy Gaetani," Greene repeated. "Do you know him?"

Eddie fidgeted on his chair. "Uh, yeah, sure," he said. "He's a good friend of mine."

"You know he's selling computers?" Pavlik asked.

Eddie shook his head nervously. "No," he said. "He didn't say anything to me about it."

The detectives looked to each other and smiled. "We'll be in touch," Greene said.

Eddie forced himself to nod again. "Sure," he said.

Pavlik turned his smile toward Eddie. "Have a nice day," he said.

CHAPTER 30

DIMI GREGOV SIPPED STOLICHNAYA FROM A PINT
bottle as he watched the blue house up the block from where he was
parked. The house was number twenty-nine, on Fairview Avenue, in
Port Washington, Long Island. It was the address that belonged to the
telephone number he had received from the black man with the gold
coins. The telephone number was under the name of Eddie and Diane
Senta.

Gregov had been in the neighborhood just over an hour. He had
moved his car frequently to avoid nosey neighbors. During one trip
around the block, Gregov noticed that the garage door at the end of the
driveway to the house was opened. The door hung crooked and seemed
jammed.

Gregov was about to get out of the car when an old man walking a
small dog knocked on his window.

"Are you looking for someone?" the old man asked.

Gregov shook his head.

"Can I help you with something?" the old man asked.

Gregov frowned at the old man. "No," he said.

"Do you live around here?" the old man asked.

Gregov started his car and waved an arm in frustration. "Fock you," he said as he pulled away from the curb.

* * * * *

Eddie turned off his telephone ringer, said his private prayer offering himself in place of his son to anything bad that might happen, and managed six solid hours of sleep. When he woke up, his pager displayed six new calls, three of them from the same number. Eddie recognized all but one of the numbers. He ignored the three calls from the same number. He called the number of the agency that he worked for and was told that he was confirmed to work the rest of the week at the same law firm where he had worked the night before. The fifth call was from his ex-wife. When Eddie called her number, he was yelled at for encouraging his son to write an essay defying the teacher's opinion on unions.

"I don't have time for this now," Eddie told his ex-wife.

"You don't have time for your son?" she yelled at him.

"Lighten up," Eddie said. "The kid is expressing himself. Leave him alone."

When his ex-wife started to yell again, Eddie hung up on her.

Eddie didn't recognize the last number on his pager. He was about to dial it when the telephone rang. Eddie picked up, said "hello," and the line went dead. He punched in *69, but the Verizon voice recording told him that the call had been made from a private number and couldn't be traced.

Eddie dialed the number on his pager and was surprised to hear Valerie Gaetani's voice.

"Val?" Eddie asked, to make sure that he had recognized her.

"Where's Tommy?" Valerie asked. Her voice was frantic.

"I don't know," Eddie said. "What do you mean?"

"He left the house yesterday afternoon, and he didn't come home yet," she said. "I assumed he was with you. The police keep calling for him, and I keep saying he isn't home, but I'm starting to get worried, Eddie. I know what happened. I think you should both. . . ."

"Whoa, whoa, whoa!" Eddie yelled into the phone. "Slow down, Val. I was working last night. The police already talked to me this morning. I told them I didn't know anything about anything."

"Well, where is he then?" Valerie Gaetani asked again. "If you don't know, where the hell is he?"

"I don't know, Val," Eddie said. "I'll see if I can find him. Talk to you later. I have to run."

Eddie hung up before Valerie Gaetani could respond again. His telephone rang a few moments later but Eddie ignored it and headed out of the house.

* * * * *

"That was fine, Mrs. Gaetani," Detective Greene said. "Thank you for your help."

Valerie Gaetani was visibly shaking. Detective Pavlik took his cell phone from her. "What does this mean?" she pleaded. "Where's Tommy?"

"We'll find him," Greene said. "I promise."

Mrs. Gaetani looked from Greene to Pavlik. "Is he all right? Is he safe?"

"We'll find him," Greene repeated.

"We will," Pavlik said.

The detectives left the Gaetani house in Corona, Queens. Valerie Gaetani had panicked about her missing husband and called the telephone numbers that they had left with her the day before. Now the detectives were second-guessing themselves as they sat in their car outside of the Gaetani home.

"We should have split up," Pavlik said. "One of us should be out in Port Washington right now following Senta."

Greene adjusted his sideview mirror. "We had the other thing to follow up on," he said.

"Then we should have sent somebody," Pavlik said. "The guy is dirty. The way he hung up on Gaetani's wife? You knew he wasn't picking up another call after that."

"Would you? We asked her to bait him. The guy had to figure we're standing beside her."

"We can still take the ride," Pavlik said. "Maybe he goes someplace and comes right back. Maybe his wife shows up, we press her."

Greene ran a thumbnail between his top front teeth. "I'm still waiting on my friend in O.C.," he said. "The guy on the Sharpetti team. Maybe Senta shows up there, we get it on tape."

Pavlik was looking at his watch. "Except if he does, O.C. isn't about to share it with us. Not after that news report about the black guy on the building surveillance tape."

"Which Eddie Senta could have heard over the news and repeated," Greene said.

"Except our girlfriend Sarah did go in with a black guy, and he did come out by himself," Pavlik said.

Greene shrugged. "Except the guys at the lab and the D.A. say that tape is useless in court. Too blurry."

"Senta claims he saw the black guy but didn't know him," Pavlik said. "Maybe the black guy knew Senta. And vice versa. Maybe they were partners."

"And something went wrong?" Greene asked. He squinted. "The brother and Eddie Senta? And what about this Tommy Gaetani slob? They all in it together and something went kabooey?"

"Kabooey?" Pavlik said as he made a face. "The O.C. unit would never give us anything on this," he added. "Not if Joe Sharp's name is in it. No way."

"Maybe we can make them give us something," Greene said. "Being a Murray Hill thing and all. Who knows."

Pavlik was looking back at the Gaetani house. He could see Mrs. Gaetani watching them from the living room window. He could tell that she was still crying. "Well, make the call," Pavlik said. "This thing is starting to bother me, especially this Eddie Senta guy. I don't like the wake of shit he leaves behind him."

Greene looked in the same direction that Pavlik was looking. "You're just a big softy," he said.

"Make the call," Pavlik said. "It's him. I know it is."

* * * * *

Singleton purchased a single ticket for Puerto Rico and settled in the motel along the Belt Parkway near Kennedy Airport. His flight was scheduled to leave the next morning at six o'clock. Singleton was planning on staying in Puerto Rico long enough to meet a connection that he had made at Fishkill Penitentiary a year earlier.

In the meantime, to kill the night, he called an escort service and ordered two women, a blonde and an Asian. He hid his cash and gold coins behind a ceiling tile in the bathroom, leaving out the price of the escorts, plus a hundred dollars for tips. He placed the .380 under the telephone book in one of the night tables and put both clips for the gun in the back of another drawer of the same night table.

Singleton sipped at a fifth of Johnny Walker Black while he waited for the escorts. He smoked marijuana from a pipe that he had made from a piece of tin foil that had previously wrapped a ham and egg sandwich. The triple-homicide investigation was already old news. At least the local stations weren't featuring the story. Halfway through the news, the only mention of the "Murray Hill Massacre" was an interview with one of the daughters of Larry Singotti at his funeral. Singleton changed the channel to watch wrestling.

CHAPTER 31

THEY WERE INSIDE OF THE CONFESSIONAL BOX AT
St. Jude's Church on Seaview Avenue in Canarsie. It was a meeting
arranged by two of Joe Sharpetti's soldiers. The church had been closed
for one hour, for a five-hundred-dollar donation.

Eddie kneeled down in the box and whispered through the screen
in the dark. "Sorry I'm late," he said. "I was waiting down the block to
make sure I wasn't being followed."

"I hope you weren't followed," Joe Sharpetti's voice responded
through the screen. "We're all better safe than sorry these days."

"I need to talk to you," Eddie said. "I'm in trouble. I need help."

"I know all about it," Sharpetti said.

"You do? How?"

"That guy does the impressions," Sharpetti said. "Tommy what's-
his-name. Your friend from Queens."

"Tommy G," Eddie said. "What did he tell you?"

"Enough," Sharpetti said. "Too much. It doesn't matter."

"I need to find this guy who did the killings," Eddie said. "I saw him
the other day. I didn't see his face, but I saw him. Some black guy. I

need to find him, or they'll nail me with this thing I had nothing to do with. I went in to take some cash and computers."

"I know all about it," Sharpetti said. "Your friend had a big mouth."

"Is there any way . . . had?" Eddie said. "What do you mean, had?"

"He's gone," Sharpetti said. "Don't even ask. It's done."

Eddie felt his stomach drop as he closed his eyes in the dark. "Jesus Christ," he said.

"He was falling to pieces," Sharpetti said. "He would have given you up to the law next. He came to me to convince you to give up. I didn't agree with him. From what I know, you're doing the right thing. Hang tough. If you need a lawyer, I'll find you one. Don't talk to the cops without one, though, trust me on that."

Eddie was still smarting from the news of Tommy Gaetani. "Jesus Christ," he repeated.

"It had to be," Sharpetti said. "I know you were friends. The guy was in over his head. He came to me for Christ sakes. Right to my front door. Nothing good would have come from letting him run around the way he was."

"He had a wife and kid," Eddie said.

"Those are the breaks," Sharpetti said. "Don't ask me to be more sympathetic than that. This is the world we deal in. When you don't belong, you don't belong."

Eddie wiped at a tear. "I can't believe how this turned out," he said. "I never should have gone through with it."

"You all right?" Sharpetti asked.

"Yeah," Eddie said. "I'm the only one still all right from all this."

"Good," Sharpetti said. "Because it's time to get over it. Now. Right now. You have to think about yourself and your friends. And I have to make sure your guilt over your missing friend doesn't spill back into my lap. You understand, right?"

"Yeah," Eddie said.

"Good," Sharpetti said. "Because I'm going to leave now. And we can't see each other for a while. A long while. I'll stay in touch through my people, but don't come looking for me. Hang around the church another few minutes, and talk to my guy when you get out. Tell him all you can about this black guy, and we'll see if we can track him down, but don't count on it. If this spook has half a brain, he's in Tahiti by now."

"There was gold involved," Eddie said. "He'll try to fence it."

"Gold?" Sharpetti said. "Then he really is a moron. Some spook convict picks up gold from a triple murder is gonna try and fence it? If he ain't in Argentina, he should be. If he tries to fence the gold here, we'll know about it. You just take care of yourself. Watch your back, and forget your friend. What's done is done."

Eddie was too numb to respond. His eyes were still tearing. He started to sniffle as Sharpetti left the confessional box. Eddie pulled at his hair as he crumpled against the wall of the confessional. He felt his body tighten with muscle cramps as he pictured Tommy Gaetani in a ditch with a hole in the back of his head.

* * * * *

Detectives Greene and Pavlik surveyed the traffic on Broadway from the steps of the criminal courts building in downtown Manhattan. Pavlik ate a frankfurter with mustard and onions. Greene picked at the salt on a pretzel.

"I hope you brought some breath mints," Greene told Pavlik. He pointed at the frankfurter Pavlik was eating.

Pavlik ignored the comment. "What our friends in the DA's office have to say?" he asked.

"Which bad news you want first?" Greene said. "There isn't enough to arrest Senta yet. There isn't even enough to warrant surveillance, unless you wanna spend the night parked up the block from his house. We can't do anything—wiretaps, surveillance or anything else—until we give Senta enough time so we can claim he's avoiding us."

"And this is because why?" Pavlik asked.

"The coroner determined it was a brother had sex with our girl, Ms. Sarah, before she caught the bullets killed her. Some form of Sickle Cell trait."

"The brother in the building surveillance tape?" Pavlik asked.

"You can't get a brother's name from a surveillance tape," Greene said. "That plus Ms. Sarah went through that lobby with five people in total. At least two of which were black."

Pavlik frowned as he took another bite from the frankfurter. "There's a film project, you want one," he said. "Figure a way to film your brethren in apartment building lobbies with enough accuracy to prosecute."

"Right," Greene said. "Thanks for showing up late again."

"I was out fishing, too," Pavlik said. "Following up your Joe Sharpetti shot with one of my own."

"And?" Greene said. "Any luck?"

"Tommy Gaetani went in Sharpetti's social club the other night," Pavlik said. "He left about an hour later with one of Joe Sharp's crew, but they weren't followed."

Greene made a face. "So Joe Sharp whacked this Tommy Gaetani for what? For Eddie Senta?"

Pavlik finished the last of the frankfurter. "My friend is federal," he said as he wiped his mouth. "He's on a RICO investigation separate from the city-organized crime squad. All he could do was verify things for me. Nothing more than that. Nothing about Eddie Senta."

"So, we don't get the end story on Tommy Gaetani until somebody flips," Greene said.

"We still have the wife," Pavlik said.

Greene shook his head. "Hearsay. Panicked wife. It was less than twenty-four hours since he disappeared when we first brought it to the D.A. Doesn't count until we substantiate it with something concrete."

"The computers."

Greene shook his head again. "They must have worn gloves when they took them," he said. "And the computers we have must have been passed around a dozen times since they were stolen."

Pavlik waved it off. "They can't stretch those phone calls Senta made to that broad for now? For a bullshit indictment? For something we can put surveillance on? Not even wiretaps?"

Greene shrugged.

"Fuck them then," Pavlik said. "What do they want, the guy to mail us his confession?"

"Something like that. It's Murray Hill. They want whatever case we make to stick."

Pavlik wiped at his mouth with the back of his hand. "Well, what about that other guy? The one from the office nobody knew who the fuck he was."

"Ivan Greenbaum," Greene said. He took a deep breath. "I'm sorry to say that the St. Thomas police are more useless than the average white man. They couldn't dig anything up we didn't already figure out from Singotti's safe deposit box. The guy was a jewel dealer on the island. He dealt in precious gems and gold but not the kind in the box."

"Which doesn't mean he didn't get Krugerrands on the black market," Pavlik said.

"Zzzactly," Greene said. "The man was dirty. No bank records. Which, when I asked another friend knows the system down there, means they already went into poor Ivan's personal bank box and removed whatever was inside it."

"The cops?" Pavlik said.

"They more crooked down there than we are up here," Greene said.

Pavlik picked between his teeth with a matchbook cover. "I gotta work on my tan," he said. "Maybe put in for a transfer."

CHAPTER 32

EDDIE EMPTIED ONE OF THREE SAFE DEPOSIT BOXES that he had kept with his mother while she was still alive. He retrieved a Smith & Wesson .38mm with two boxes of bullets and a shoebox with thirty thousand dollars in cash. He took the cash to his ex-wife in Brooklyn, where he set the shoebox full of fifty- and hundred-dollar bills on the kitchen table while his ex-wife poured coffee.

"Are you really in trouble?" Maryanne Senta asked Eddie. She was a youthful thirty-six years old. Her black hair was cut short. She had just come out of the shower and was still wearing her robe.

"I think so," Eddie said. "But I can't explain it yet. Just take this money and find someplace safe for it. Not here in the house. Somewhere nobody can get to it. A safe deposit box in your bank is a good place. Let your mother cosign the box for you. And don't use the money, Maryanne. It's for emergencies. For you and Jack. Don't go blow it someplace on furniture or some shit."

His ex-wife had been preparing to go to work. Her makeup was spread out at one end of the kitchen table. She picked up an orange shade of lipstick. "I can use a few dollars, Eddie," she said. "Things are tight here."

Eddie placed his hands over the money. "No," he said. "Not yet. Not unless it's an emergency."

"And what about if you're not around to bring us money?" she asked with anger.

"I'll be around," he said. "And if I'm not, I'll make provisions, don't worry. Keep this separate for now. In the case of a real emergency. Put it away."

Maryanne pushed an ashtray in front of Eddie when he lit a cigarette. "You want to stay here for a few days?" she asked.

"Not with Jack around, no," Eddie said. "I don't want him to know any of this shit yet. Maybe nothing will happen, and he can be spared."

"What is it?"

"I can't tell you."

"Where will you go?"

"Motels. Friends. I'll be all right. I just need a few days to help myself. I need to find somebody."

Maryanne Senta leaned forward on her chair. "What if something happens? I mean for Jack. What do I tell him?"

Eddie shook his head. "I don't know," he said. "Just don't tell him anything yet."

Maryanne leaned back again. "I know that look, Eddie. What are you going to do?"

"I won't sit around and wait," Eddie said. "I won't do that."

* * * * *

"You have party, don't invite us," Dimi Gregov said to James Singleton.

They were facing each other in the motel doorway. Singleton was dressed in his underwear and a red tank top. Gregov was wearing a black windbreaker over a white T-shirt. Singleton was bleary-eyed. His pupils shrank from the sunlight.

"Hey, man, what's up?" Singleton said, once he recognized the Russian. "Come on in."

The Russian stepped into the motel room and saw that it was a mess. "Two girls for one man," Gregov said. "You must have big cock."

"You know what they say about the black man," Singleton said. He grabbed the pair of jeans on the dresser and pulled them on.

"You pay how much for girls?" Gregov asked Singleton.

Singleton laughed off the question. "They should have paid me," he said. "Hundred each, with a tip. You want, I can call them back. They from a service."

Gregov held his nose. "After black man? No thanks."

"You don't have to go down for a taste, my man," Singleton said. "You could let them polish your knob."

Gregov sat on a chair at a small table. "Vear you get gold, black man?" he asked.

Singleton made a face. "I told you, my partner," he said. "The guy I gave you his telephone number. Eddie Senta."

Gregov lit a cigarette. "Vhy you vant him dead?"

"I don't want him anything," Singleton said. "The man tried to rob me. You want the gold, go get it. You don't, that's okay, too. Hey, you watching me? That how you knew about the girls?"

Gregov blew smoke at Singleton. "Maybe you have gold," he said.

"You think I'd be here?" Singleton asked. "Maybe stupid runs in your family. You and stupid Victor."

Gregov stared at Singleton. "You come vit me and Victor to your partner," he said.

"Victor, too, now, huh? I guess he out after all."

"Vee go all three of us," Gregov said. "In case your partner don't have gold. Then I kill you, too."

Singleton glared at Gregov. "Yeah and maybe I kill you," he said.

"You and that numb-nuts cousin of yours. Do a man a favor, and this is how you get treated."

Gregov smiled. "Get dressed," he said.

Singleton pointed to the door. "Yeah, well, you can give me half an hour," he said. "I want to take a shower, and no, you can't wait here for me. You were watching me from wherever. Go back and watch some more."

Gregov watched as Singleton stepped into the bathroom. He frowned when the black man closed the door. He heard the shower water running and stood up from the bed. He gave a quick look around the room from where he was standing and left.

* * * * *

Jack Senta used the computers at Canarsie High School to print out the opera paper that he wrote for his punishment. It was a paper that defended the concept of vengeance, and it had upset his mother. He decided to surprise his father by delivering the paper on the opera, *Rigoletto*, along with a gift CD of aria highlights after school.

Jack called his mother from the high school after his last class, but she had already left for work. He left a message that he was taking the subway into the city, where he would get the Long Island Railroad out to Port Washington. He was going to see his father and would call her at work later.

Jack walked to the Rockaway Parkway train station and sat in the last car. He opened the opera CD he had bought for his father and gave it a listen during the first leg of his journey. He read along from the libretto as Luciano Pavarotti belted out *Questa o Quella.*

* * * * *

"I don't like sitting up front," Singleton said.

They were on the Belt Parkway heading east toward Long Island. Victor drove a stolen Ford Taurus, while Singleton sat in front and Gregov sat in the back behind Victor.

"Don't vorry," Gregov said. "I von't shoot you in car."

Singleton turned in his seat. "Do I look worried?"

"The Cross Island or the Southern State?" Victor asked his cousin. He looked in the rearview mirror at his cousin for an answer.

"Cross Island," Gregov said. "Stay in left lane."

"You been there already?" Singleton asked.

Gregov didn't answer.

"Fine, motherfucker," Singleton said. He spoke at Victor. "Your cousin needs to learn some manners, huh, Vic?"

"Is business," Victor said. "Serious person. I told you in Fishkill. Dimi is serious person."

Singleton glanced over his shoulder at Gregov. "What he is, is full of himself," he said. "And he not the first person I met like that. Full of himself and full of shit at the same time. You know what I mean, Vic? You remember guys like that in the joint. Talk a lot of shit until push come to shove. Then what they do is fall short."

"Shut up, black man," Gregov said. "You give me headache."

"I was talking to Vic," Singleton said.

"You talk too much," Gregov said.

"To make up for you, Holmes," Singleton said.

Gregov pulled a .9mm Beretta from a shoulder holster inside of his windbreaker and pointed it at Singleton. "Now you shut up, okay?" he said.

Singleton smiled. "I was just thinking what we need is the radio," he said. "Some tunes, right, Vic?"

Victor turned on the radio. An oldies station played the Temptations singing "My Girl." Gregov holstered the gun and looked out the window. Singleton rocked his head side to side in time with the music.

CHAPTER 33

EDDIE DROVE TO A MOTEL ON SUNRISE HIGHWAY IN Rockville Center. He paid for a room and tried to place a call with his cell phone, but the battery was low. The phone beeped a few times and died. He left the room and drove a few blocks away to a pay phone outside of a diner.

"Did you follow up on the black guy I told you about?" Eddie asked Detective Greene.

"Yes, we did," Greene said. "The woman, Sarah Parker, had sex with a black man within forty-eight hours of her murder. Where are you?"

"That was her new boyfriend," Eddie said. "The one I told you about."

"It was a blood test, but it doesn't identify who the black man was," Greene said. "Where are you now?"

"What about the thing on the news?" Eddie asked. "The surveillance camera."

"Inconclusive," Greene said. "It wouldn't mean a signed confession anyway. Where are you?"

"The guy was a convict," Eddie said. "Did you follow up on that?"

"Mr. Senta, where are you?" Greene asked. "I think we should sit down again and talk."

"Thanks," Eddie said and hung up.

* * * * *

Greene frowned as he hung up. "I just got played," he said.

Pavlik was forking french fries off of a paper plate. He spoke as he chewed. "What do you think he's up to?"

"Looking for the brother," Greene said.

"I was gonna ask you that," Pavlik said. "If you still call a perp a brother once you know he's a perp."

"If his skin's the right color," Greene said.

Pavlik swallowed a mouthful of fries, took a gulp of Coke from a can, and wiped at his mouth with the back of his wrist. "I gotta tell you, partner," he said. "Maybe we got it the wrong way. If this guy Senta can find the brother, then maybe they did this thing together. Could be Senta's out looking for the brother to tie up loose ends."

Greene placed his cell phone in its belt holder. "Except I don't really believe the brother'd be looking for Senta if the brother's the one did the killing," he said. "Why bother? If he already got whatever cash was involved, I gotta believe he'd be a content brother. He'd be on the next flight out of the country."

"Maybe," Pavlik said. He forked another fry off the plate. "Except maybe they did it together and each is afraid of the other doing the fingering."

* * * * *

Eddie called his wife's office number from the pay phone to leave a message. When Diane's voice mail answered, Eddie hung up. He started to call Valerie Gaetani but couldn't finish dialing the number. He called a gambling customer instead. Abraham Cohen was a jeweler in the Diamond Exchange in Chinatown. He had sold Eddie the diamond engagement ring that Diane wore.

"You getting married again?" Cohen asked, once he recognized Eddie's voice.

"Not me," Eddie said. "Never again, my friend."

"Never say never," Cohen said.

"I do need a favor, though."

"You want to move a nice Rolex, right?"

"You know me better 'n that, Abe," Eddie said. "I pay cash, I collect cash. You're the one in the buy and sell business."

"You have a point," Cohen said. "What is it I can do for you?"

"Information on gold," Eddie said. "Krugerrands, I think. How would a guy sell them here in the city? Fence them, I mean. How would a guy do that?"

"Depends," Cohen said. "How hot are they?"

"Very," Eddie said. "Or they will be soon enough."

"Then it would be difficult," Cohen said. "You should know that. It would be very difficult."

"What about where?" Eddie asked. "Where would a guy go to hawk a price?"

"Depends on who he is," Cohen said. "And on other things. Depends."

Eddie's pager vibrated against his hip. "Hold on a second," he said into the telephone. Eddie checked the number on the pager. "A black guy," Eddie continued. "A black guy just got out of the joint, did something hot enough to be in the papers. Where would a guy like that go to fence gold coins?"

"Mars, if he had any brains," Cohen said. "But a guy like that sounds like he don't have any in the first place. Or they're scrambled. He'd go dirty is my guess. He'd go underground. He'd go ethnic, again depending on who he is, who he knows."

"Suppose he knows people from inside the joint?" Eddie asked.

"I'd think that he'd go with what he knows," Cohen said. "If he knows Dominicans, he'd go to them. If he knew Italians, he'd go there. And so on."

"Thanks, Abe," Eddie said.

"What are you thanking me for? I didn't tell you anything."

"Maybe you did," Eddie said. "I'll let you know."

* * * * *

When Eddie called the telephone number that showed on his pager, George Waters answered on the first ring.

"It's Eddie, George."

"I have a short list for you."

Eddie grabbed a pen and used the back of his wife's business card for paper. "Shoot," he said.

"Singleton, James," Waters said.

Eddie waited for more. "That's it?"

"From what I'm reading of this, yeah. The man was in with a confidential folder. That means federal. Usually undercover because he's still working. Robbery is the record showing, but that don't mean anything when the folder is marked confidential. They use something vague everybody involved can remember. He was upstate in Fishkill. Did most of his time with a Russian cellmate. Guy from Brooklyn, Victor Ilynich. Ilynich is a gopher for the Russian boys down in Seagate, Brooklyn. This boy of yours smells, Eddie. I'd be careful, I was you."

"What makes you think it's this guy and nobody else?" Eddie asked.

"He fuckin' with you, he's fuckin' with the mob," Waters said. "The only people bold enough to fuck with the mob are guys already under protection. You dig?"

"About how tall is this Singleton guy? Do you have that kind of information?"

"Six-two, one-ninety-eight," Waters said. "Nasty-ass scar on his neck compliments of the Fishkill welcoming committee."

"Thanks, George," Eddie said. "I'll get you your money pronto."

"Just be careful, kid," Waters said. "Like I said, this boy smells."

"I hear you, George."

"Eddie? He smells bad."

CHAPTER 34

EDDIE USED THE PAY PHONE TO CALL DETECTIVE Greene one more time. He waited through four rings before a voice mail system picked up. Eddie looked around before talking into the machine.

"James Singleton," he said. "That's the James who killed Sarah and her boss and the other guy. He was upstate in Fishkill before they moved him to Riker's before he was released. He roomed with some Russian dude, and he's probably under Federal protection. Now I did your job for you, maybe you can concentrate on finding this guy before he kills another three people."

Eddie hung up and immediately called Diane at her office. This time he left a message.

"It's me," he said into the telephone. "I think I found the guy who did the killings. I already called it in to the police. In the meantime, stay away from the house in case the cops come bothering you. I'll keep trying until I get you."

* * * * *

Diane left the few bags that she had bothered to take out of the car in the front room of the house. She turned on a few lights and checked the telephone for messages. She saw the light blinking but didn't play the messages back. She opened the rear door of the house to let in fresh air. She opened a few windows in the dining room and den and then headed upstairs.

Diane changed into workout clothes when she was finished in the bathroom. She looked around the bedroom and found herself staring at a picture of Eddie and her wearing sunglasses in Las Vegas together. She looked from the picture to the full-length mirror against one wall. She stared at herself a long time before the doorbell interrupted her thoughts.

* * * * *

After stopping for a late lunch at a diner on Northern Boulevard, Victor drove around Eddie Senta's neighborhood a few times to familiarize himself with the streets. He made a final pass in front of the house and turned left at the corner. He drove one block and turned right, continuing to the entrance to a small shopping area behind a Mobil gas station on Port Washington Boulevard. Victor parked in the most secluded area of the lot, far away from the stores and well behind the gas station.

"We sticking out like sore thumbs," Singleton said. "This neighborhood is a bad choice to joy ride around, comrades."

"You see gas station over there?" Dimi asked. He was pointing to the Mobil station.

"Yeah, I see it," Singleton said. "And we parked over here."

"I have to pee," Victor said.

"You couldn't go at the diner, huh?" Singleton asked. "That would've been too easy, right?"

"Shut up, black man," Dimi said. He tapped Victor on the back. "Go pee," Dimi said. "I wait here."

"What about me?" Singleton asked.

"Go in your pants," Dimi said.

* * * * *

"That's a lot of information to be made up from thin air," Greene said.

They were driving east on the Long Island Expressway. Pavlik checked a map that he had spread out on his lap. Eddie Senta's address was scrawled on the top right-hand corner of the map. Pavlik circled the town of Port Washington with a red pen.

"Maybe the guy did his research," Greene said. "Which suggests he knows a lot more than we do."

"A lot more than he told us," Pavlik said. "The guy is under federal protection, this Singleton, then it makes for a whole other mess. They'll never cooperate, the feds. Even my friend, his hands were tied. He wouldn't give me names."

"They can't look away from a triple homicide," Greene said.

Pavlik folded the map in half. "They can if they want to," he said. "I've seen them do it before. Between the wiseguys and drug dealers who flip, probably ten percent of the states of Arizona and New Mexico, places like that, are guys in the program. If they need somebody to make a case, the feds, they break the rules, end of story. They look the other way without blinking, my friend. It's the nature of the beast. What was it, nineteen kills they dealt away with that one guy, Sammy the Snitch?"

Greene spotted an opening in the right lane and switched lanes. "Deals with the devils," he said.

"At the expense of the citizenry," Pavlik said.

Greene made a face. "Citizenry? What the fuck is that?"

Pavlik turned to Greene. "Oh, just the white people," he said. "It wouldn't concern you."

* * * * *

"Jack!" Diane exclaimed when she saw Eddie's son at the front door. She let him in the house just as the telephone rang.

Diane ushered her stepson into the living room as she answered the cordless telephone.

"Hello?" Diane said into the telephone. "Hello?"

The caller hung up. She rolled her eyes at Jack Senta and shook her head. "Probably kids."

* * * * *

Dimi was using his cell phone. He dialed a number, listened for a few seconds, and then turned off the power. He leaned forward and handed his cousin the Beretta.

"If black man comes out without me, kill him," Dimi told his cousin.

"Just like that, huh?" Singleton asked.

"Just like that," Dimi said.

Singleton looked into Victor's blue eyes. "You gonna shoot me, Victor?"

"If you come out alone, yes," Victor said.

Dimi pulled a second gun from an ankle strap. He showed it to Singleton. "Gold better be there, black man," he said.

Singleton eyed the weapon. "I hear you," he said.

"Wait ten minutes, and drive to house," Dimi told his cousin. "Wait off corner. Look at newspaper."

Singleton smiled. "He can't read it, can he?"

"Fock you," Victor said.

"Get out," Dimi told Singleton.

Singleton stepped out of the car at the same time as Dimi. They both walked back up the street toward Eddie Senta's house.

* * * * *

When Eddie finally reached Diane, she was at the house. Diane answered the phone sounding annoyed.

"Yes, who is it?"

"Diane, it's me!" Eddie said. "I've been trying to get you the last couple of hours. I called you at work a dozen times."

"Somebody just called and hung up," she said. "Was that you?"

"No," Eddie said. "I've been calling your office."

"I didn't check my messages," Diane said. "Jack is here. Where are you?"

"Jack?" Eddie said. "What's Jack doing there?"

"He brought you the opera paper he was writing."

"Oh," Eddie said.

"Where are you?" Diane asked again.

"Close," Eddie said. "But I can't come home yet. I found the guy who killed Sarah and her boss. I already called the cops, but I had to leave a voice message. The cops will probably be there any minute looking for me."

"Huh?" Diane said. "Wait, I think they're here now. Someone is at the front door. Hold on."

"Shit," Eddie said. He listened a full minute before he heard what sounded like a smack followed by his son's voice screaming a curse word.

"Fuck!" Eddie yelled on his end of the line. He called his house again, but the phone rang without anyone picking up. He dropped the telephone and sprinted for the Dodge.

CHAPTER 35

IMI HAD SINGLETON SHOVE HIS WAY INTO THE
house when the woman answered the door. When the woman tried to
push back, Dimi smacked her hard across the face. She fell backward
onto the floor.

A young kid stood up from a chair in the next room and cursed at
both men. Singleton grabbed the kid by a shoulder and spun him
around. He used his right hand to muffle the kid's mouth.

Dimi showed the woman the .22mm he was holding. He had her
shut the blinds and lock the front door.

"She a good looking woman," Singleton said. He was looking the
woman up and down as he continued to muffle the kid's mouth.

"Get up," Dimi told the woman. "Inside." He waved the gun toward
the living room.

"Don't hurt him," the woman told Singleton. Her voice was
shaking.

"That be up to you, sweetheart," Singleton said.

"Veer is gold?" Dimi asked the woman.

The woman looked from Singleton to Dimi. "What gold?" she asked.

Dimi looked to Singleton. Singleton frowned. "Give me ten minutes with her, and we have the gold and a couple blow jobs," he said.

The woman trembled. "Please, don't," she begged. "Please."

Dimi checked his watch. "Veer is focking gold?" he asked the woman again.

* * * * *

An FBI surveillance van disguised as a florist's delivery van parked half a block behind the stolen Ford Taurus. The driver pulled down on the white cap he was wearing. Special Agent Eugene Morris and two other Special Agents, both white men in their mid-thirties, prepared to exit the van. All three agents wore black windbreakers with gold lettering across the back identifying them as FBI.

"The way this goes down is simple," Morris told the other two agents. "We don't kill the Russian. Under no circumstances do we kill the Russian. He's the one that isn't black, in case you get confused."

"What if he fires at us?" one of the agents asked.

"Shoot him in the legs," Morris said. "Don't kill him." He leaned forward on the front seat to look out the window. "Can you hear pretty clear with the windows open?" he asked the driver.

"Better if I move up some more," the driver said. "I might not hear a gunshot from here."

"We'll give them a few minutes," Morris said. "Once they come out, we'll assume somebody inside is dead."

"Don't we want to stop that?" the driver asked.

"Not necessarily," Morris said. He racked the slide on his Beretta .9mm.

* * * * *

"This is a pretty neighborhood," Detective Greene said. They had just turned off the Long Island Expressway and were driving north on Port Washington Boulevard. "Nice place for a black family to relocate, don't you think?" Greene asked.

Detective Pavlik was rubbing his knuckles. "It's going to rain," he said. "My knuckles are sore."

"You're spending too much time in the bathroom with those magazines," Greene said.

"I'm serious," Pavlik said. "It's gonna pour." He leaned forward to look up at the sky. "Black clouds," he said. "This arthritis is getting fucking serious."

As they crossed Northern Boulevard, Greene glanced at the private entrance to a condominium development. "They should reshoot *American Beauty* right here," he said. "A black version. Vanessa Williams and Danny Glover. Play the irony angle."

"Hell, use that model, Tyra Banks, and call it *Black Beauty*," Pavlik said.

Greene wrinkled his nose. "She a sellout," he said. "Besides, not enough meat on that girl. She might as well be white."

Pavlik was looking at a map of Port Washington. "Senta's place is up about another mile. Couple blocks from the police station."

"See what I mean about the irony angle?" Greene said.

"I'm starting to believe this is a big waste of time," Pavlik said. "The time for us to have been here was yesterday. Especially if the feds are involved with this Singleton."

"It's the best we can do while they run a check on the information Senta left us," Greene said. "We don't know for sure the feds are involved. Maybe it was misdirection, Senta's call."

"What I was saying," Pavlik said. "Maybe Senta's message buys him just enough time to hop a flight somewhere."

"Then again, maybe the wife is home," Greene proposed. "Maybe she has something to say. Maybe she knows something about Senta and Sarah Parker."

"Maybe we could fill her in, see what happens," Pavlik said.

Greene flinched. "Oooh, you a nasty S.O.B., you don't like somebody."

"You're right about that," Pavlik said. "I don't like this Senta character. I don't like him one bit."

Greene spotted a bagel shop in a small shopping area set back off Port Washington Boulevard. He pointed at the name of the place. "In the meantime, that's where Danny Glover can get his minimum wage job," he said. "That bagel shop there, Let There Be Bagels. Then the wife, Vanessa, comes in with her boyfriend's hand planted on her fine ass and Danny says, 'Can I help you?'"

Pavlik set the map down. "It's two blocks up from here," he said. "Fairview Avenue. Between Orchard and Elm."

Greene glanced to his left at a cemetery. "Orchard and Elm?" Greene asked. "Nice touch. Freddie Kruger meets the African American beauty. The irony in this piece is killer."

Pavlik shook his head. "You got rocks in your fuckin' head," he said. "The irony is killer."

* * * * *

"Who the fuck are they?" the Special Agent behind the steering wheel asked.

"Cops," Agent Morris said. He stepped between the seats into the back of the van. "City cops. And what they're doing here is one question I don't think I want answered right now."

"What do we do?" the Special Agent in the back of the van asked.

"You both wait here," Morris said. "Watch our friend Victor." He pulled the handle on the van's side door and slid the door back. "I'll go and see what the fuck this is all about."

CHAPTER 36

H

E HAD NEVER KILLED ANYONE IN HIS LIFE. THE
closest he had come was the night that a lone assassin had attempted to
kill Joe Sharpetti at the strip club. The gunman, surprised by Eddie's
sudden appearance, had turned his gun on Eddie and fired two shots.
Eddie had actually heard one of the shots whistle past his right ear.
Then Eddie had used a powerful forearm shiver to the throat to knock
the gunman off balance. The gunman had nearly choked to death from
the blow.

The entire sequence of events that night in the strip club had been
a series of events strewn together by chance. From the time that Eddie
had emerged from the men's room just a few feet from where the
gunman had stood firing at Joe Sharpetti's table, to the bullets
whistling past his ear, to the forearm shiver, everything had been pure
chance and circumstance.

Now it was different. Now, if his son and his wife were in danger,
Eddie was prepared to kill with intent.

When Eddie spotted the two detectives crossing his front lawn, he
turned left on Fairview Avenue and parked at the corner of Orchard

Street. The rain started to fall as he zipped the black windbreaker that he was wearing. He shoved his gun inside the waist of his pants and covered it with the bottom of his windbreaker.

Eddie circled around through a neighbor's yard to the back of his house. He could see the detectives standing in the driveway trying to look through the side window. He crouched down to remain hidden from sight, but the sound of a gunshot brought him straight up. He saw both detectives pull their guns as they flattened against the wall of the house.

* * * * *

"That vas varning, black man," Dimi said. He had just shot a hole into the back of the headboard of the king-sized bed.

They were upstairs in the master bedroom. The woman had crawled into the space between the bed and her secretary. She covered her chest with one arm and held on to the boy with the other. Both the woman and the boy were shaking.

Singleton held the woman's torn workout top in his right hand. He was frozen from the shot that the Russian had just fired. "You got to be crazy, shooting that gun in here," Singleton said.

"Next time I shoot you," Dimi said. He aimed the gun at Singleton's chest.

"You gonna do that, you better use a muffler," Singleton said. "This a white neighborhood, comrade, in case you didn't notice. Somebody probably already called that first shot in."

"Veer is gold?" Dimi asked Singleton.

"Take it easy," Singleton said. "Her husband's the one took the gold. Maybe he didn't tell her about it."

Dimi glanced at his watch. He moved to the back window and could see someone approaching the back of the house. "That husband?" he asked the woman. He waved the gun toward the window. "Come, look," he told her.

* * * * *

Eddie was looking through the back window into the den when Detective Greene spotted him.

"Hey, get the fuck down!" Greene whispered.

Eddie took a long look inside but didn't see anything.

"Get down!" Greene repeated.

Eddie shot the detective a dirty look. "My wife and kid are in there," he told Greene. "I called her before, and she said somebody was at the door. They hung up on me."

Suddenly Pavlik appeared behind Greene. "Singleton?" he asked.

Eddie wiped sweat from his forehead. "I have no idea," he said. "But I'm not waiting down here anymore."

Eddie started for the door. Greene cut him off. "Hold on, cowboy," Greene said. "This is our gig."

"Correction, it's ours," another voice said.

All three men looked toward the driveway, where a stocky man crouched, a gun in one hand and an open identification wallet in the other. "FBI," the stocky man said. "Special Agent Morris."

* * * * *

Diane hugged Jack tight against her. She leaned forward to shield her stepson from the Russian's sight.

"I'm afraid," Jack whispered.

"Me, too," she whispered back.

"Where's Dad?" Jack asked her.

Then the Russian told her to get up and look into the yard. She didn't want to leave Jack, but she had no choice. She was pushed in front of the window and told to identify her husband. She saw Eddie and two other men when the Russian poked her hard in the ribs.

"Is husband?" the Russian asked her.

"I don't see him," she told the Russian. "I see somebody else. Two men. Three now."

The Russian shoved her away from the window to see for himself. Diane tried to signal her stepson with her eyes, but the boy was looking toward the doorway.

* * * * *

"Who you here for?" Pavlik asked the federal agent.

"The Russian," Agent Morris said.

All four men were leaning against the house. Greene was closest to the yard end of the house. Eddie was between Greene and Pavlik. Morris was at the extreme end nearest the street.

"Singleton is our hook," Morris continued.

"Singleton is our murder suspect," Greene said. "Three people in Murray Hill. Maybe you read about it."

"I don't have time for a debate," Morris said. "Singleton is under federal protection, end of story."

"Not for murder, he isn't," Pavlik said.

"Until he's convicted he is. Now, please stay back. Assist if you'd like, but I go in first." The sound of sirens suddenly filled the streets. "Who the hell is that?" Morris asked.

"The locals, probably," Greene said. "There were shots fired."

"I hope you have a speech for them, too," Pavlik told Morris.

The three law enforcement officers looked at each other as the sirens grew louder. Eddie said "Fuck you" to the lot of them and dashed around Greene through the back door of the house.

CHAPTER 37

THE SOUND OF SIRENS FILLED THE STREETS. Singleton tossed the woman her torn workout top and put his hands on his hips.

"Nice going, Demi," he said.

Dimi stood flattened against the wall alongside the bedroom window. "There are three of them outside," he said. "Bring me boy."

"No!" the woman yelled. "Use me," she said. "Please."

"Fucking cowards," the boy said.

"You best shut the fuck up, kid," Singleton said.

Dimi pulled the woman up by the hair. He stood behind her as he looked down into the yard.

"They coming in," Dimi said. "Three of them."

"And another hundred out the front, I'm sure," Singleton said.

"Go see," Dimi told Singleton.

"I don't think so," Singleton said.

Dimi waved the gun at Singleton. "Go, motherfocker," he said.

Singleton heard somebody on the stairs outside of the bedroom and stepped further away from the path to the doorway. "I think we got company," he said.

Dimi ignored Singleton. He was focused on the activity directly below the window. He could see the three men entering the house: a tall white man and two black men. One wore a jacket with "FBI" on the back.

"Focking shit," Dimi said.

"Yeah, remind me to thank your cousin for the warning," Singleton said.

* * * * *

Victor pressed the power button on the cell phone one more time when he heard a popping sound from inside of the house. They had been inside more than fifteen minutes when the two cops parked in front of the house. Victor had tried the cell phone three times already. When the black man wearing the FBI jacket followed the two cops onto the driveway, Victor prepared to make a run for it. He racked the slide on his gun just in case. He checked his rearview mirror when he thought he saw something move in the passenger's sideview mirror. When he turned to his right on the front seat, Victor's eyes opened wide with shock. A young white man pointed a gun directly at Victor's head.

"Oh, shit," Victor said.

"Freeze!" the white man said. "FBI!"

"Hands up!" another voice said. "Touch the roof."

The second voice also sounded white, but Victor didn't bother to look and see. He raised his hands above his head slowly until he felt the roof of the car.

* * * * *

When the black man backed away from the doorway, Jack Senta

thought that he could make it out of the bedroom. He watched the Russian, who was holding his stepmother by her hair. The Russian seemed focused on whatever was going on in the yard.

Jack scrambled to his feet and was on his way when he heard the bang behind him. He felt a piercing pain in his left leg, and his body hurtled forward. He banged his face hard against the carpeted floor in the hallway. For a split second, Jack thought that he saw his father standing in the hallway. His vision was blurry. Then he heard another bang behind him. He thought that he heard his stepmother scream. Then everything suddenly went dark.

* * * * *

Eddie was in the middle of mouthing his private prayer when he saw his son's face strike the floor in the hallway. Eddie knew Jack had been shot. He immediately grabbed his son by the shirt and dragged him out of the doorway into the hallway. He was about to drag Jack into the next room when he heard Diane scream.

Eddie took a deep breath, bit his lower lip, and stepped into the master bedroom doorway in a firing stance, extending the gun ahead of him as he crouched. For the second time in his life, bullets whistled past Eddie's right ear. He could see a tall blond man shooting at him from directly across the bedroom. He could see Diane on her knees being held by her hair. Eddie heard Diane scream again. He fired back at the blonde man, two shots in quick succession. The blond man slammed off the wall directly behind him before falling forward on his face.

* * * * *

Detective Pavlik was up the stairs first. He held his Glock in his right hand as he peered over the top of the stairway. The bedrooms were off to the left. He could see a boy stretched out on his stomach on the floor in the hallway, bleeding from the back of his left leg. Pavlik immediately pulled the boy back to the stairs. He handed the boy off to Detective Greene.

Agent Morris stepped up ahead of Pavlik. He held his Beretta out in front of him as he made his way down the short hallway at the top of the stairs. He yelled, "FBI! Throw your weapons into the hallway!"

* * * * *

Singleton had just taken his own weapon out of his pants when he saw the huge blood stain on Dimi's chest. He tossed his gun on the floor, dropped down, and covered the back of his head with both hands. "Don't shoot!" he yelled. "Don't shoot!"

When Singleton heard the sound of a familiar voice in the hallway, he called back. "It's Jimmy in here. Don't fucking shoot!"

* * * * *

She had heard the shots and screamed from instinct. She was sure that her stepson was wounded. Then she saw the black man with the gun. Then she heard more shots. Eddie was suddenly in the doorway. Diane screamed again.

The Russian had let go of her hair. Diane fell to the floor. She rolled away from the Russian toward the wall. When she turned back, she saw a look of pain on the Russian's face. She saw him drop his gun. He banged into the wall behind him, and she could see the blood through his white T-shirt. She saw his eyes glaze as he fell forward. Diane moved further away when the Russian struck the floor a few feet from her.

When she turned away from the Russian, Diane saw Eddie again. She called his name.

* * * * *

Eddie stepped into the room and saw the black man flat on his stomach on the floor, with his hands on the back of his head. Eddie spotted the gun on the floor and kicked it further away from the black man. He helped his wife up off the floor and motioned her toward the hallway.

"Jack was shot in the leg," Eddie told Diane. "He's in the hallway. There are cops out there. FBI, too. Go."

Diane quickly sidestepped the black man on the floor. "Eddie?" she asked before stepping out of the room.

"Close the door," Eddie told her.

* * * * *

Agent Morris was about to step into the bedroom when he saw the woman. He stepped back in the hallway and removed his FBI jacket. He draped the jacket over the woman's shoulders as he guided her toward Detective Pavlik, who took the woman back to the stairs.

"What's going on?" Morris asked the woman.

The woman was trembling. All she could do was shake her head.

"FBI!" Morris yelled again. "We're coming inside!"

Agent Morris started toward the master bedroom one more time when a gunshot stopped him in his tracks. "Shit," he said.

* * * * *

Eddie had fired a shot into the ceiling to keep the FBI and police out of the bedroom. He looked down at the black man on the floor. "You Singleton?" he asked. "You the one killed Sarah?"

"No way," the black man answered. "I ain't killed nobody."

"James Singleton!" a voice yelled from the hallway. "This is the FBI! We're coming in!"

Eddie stood over the black man he now knew was James Singleton. "Did you kill Sarah?" he asked again.

"This is the FBI!" the voice yelled again. "Toss your weapons in the hallway!"

Singleton smiled. "I'm with them, boss," he told Eddie.

"I know," Eddie said.

Singleton lost his smile. "What you mean, you know?"

Eddie kicked Singleton in the shoulder. "Did you kill her?" he asked.

"Don't kick me, motherfucker!" Singleton said. He was showing teeth.

"Did you give her a chance?" Eddie asked. "The cops said it was an execution."

"This is the FBI!" the voice yelled one more time. "Toss your weapons in the hallway now!"

Singleton smiled at Eddie one more time. Eddie smiled back as he cocked the revolver. Singleton lost his smile a second time. He looked to the gun on the rug a full six feet away.

"It's not like you don't have a chance," Eddie said. "I don't even know there are any bullets left."

Singleton looked from the gun to the bedroom door to Eddie.

"Go for it," Eddie said.

Singleton hesitated a split second before he gave a quick look back at the bedroom door to try and distract Eddie. Eddie moved his head in the direction of Singleton's glance, but he never took his eyes off of the black man. Singleton started to scramble on all fours when Eddie yelled, "Stop!"

Singleton dove across the floor toward the gun. He reached for it as he looked up at Eddie one more time. Singleton could see Eddie's teeth were clenched beyond the extended gun. Singleton hesitated a split second before he grabbed the gun with his right hand. As he turned toward Eddie with the gun, Singleton could see the flash in the barrel of Eddie's weapon just before the first of two bullets entered his right eye.

"I said stop," Eddie said.

CHAPTER 38

ETECTIVE GREENE TRIED TO LIST THE FACTS OF THE
latest homicide case while eating lunch at Umberto's Clam Bar on
Broome Street in Little Italy. Detective Pavlik was inattentive.

"The wife made videotapes of her affairs," Greene said as he
counted off his fingers. "The husband discovers the tapes, he recog-
nizes one of the lovers, he goes after them both."

Pavlik stabbed at a fried calamari ring sitting on top of his
spaghetti. Greene sprinkled lemon on a clam and pointed to a marinara
sauce stain on Pavlik's white shirt.

"Fuck," Pavlik said. He dipped his napkin in the glass of water and
wiped at the stain.

"He's humiliated, the husband," Greene said. "Who can blame
him? So he kills her and the one she's with."

Pavlik was still dabbing at the stain. "Too bad she didn't kill herself," he said.

"And he films it," Greene continued. "Then he gets nervous, he
realizes what he did, and he takes the tape with him." He stopped just
before sucking the clam off the shell. "Where?" he asked himself.

"France," Pavlik said. "Maybe somewhere in the South Pacific. Who the fuck cares? Not me. Not right now."

Pavlik chewed on squid tentacles as he speared another ring of calamari. He looked down at the stain on his shirt and mumbled under his breath. He tried wiping at the stain one more time.

"You should've ordered something without sauce," Greene said.

"Yeah, well, it's too late now," Pavlik said. He gave up trying to clean the stain. "I have a date tonight. The one fucking night I need a clean shirt."

"This the Irish gangster's sister?" Greene asked. "Your date this evening."

"Aelish," Pavlik said, trying an Irish accent. "Aelish Phalen. A lovely lass from the Emerald Isle."

Greene sucked the last of his raw clams and wiped his mouth with a paper napkin. "I forget how romantic you can be," he said. "You gonna pick up a six-pack, some potato chips for this date?"

"I'm taking her to an Italian joint out in Port Washington, believe it or not. Where we had that little mess with the feds and one of their protected witnesses. A friend of mine says this place is excellent." He pulled a business card from his wallet and read it. "Montebello's."

"A Polack takes a Mick to a Guinea joint," Greene said. "Sounds lovely."

"You don't want to be pickin' on the Irish now, boy-oh," Pavlik said, trying the brogue again.

Greene popped a small soup cracker into his mouth. "And why's that?" he asked.

"Her brother, for one thing," Pavlik said, returning to his normal voice. "Peter Phalen has held hands with more than a few of New York's finest. He's what they used to call a respectable gangster. Looks after his own."

"The Mick cops over in Sunnyside Gardens," Greene said.

"Billy Murphy, in particular."

"Billy Murphy. So, they stick together. Big deal."

"Phalen is the man I went to see about the computers," Pavlik added. "He's been willing and able to help a cop or two in the past. Even those of a superior ethnicity. Not to mention he knows damn near every fence in this city. Peter Phalen is a man in touch with many different worlds."

Greene wiped his forehead with the back of his wrist. "What's this got to do with Billy Murphy?" he asked.

Pavlik stretched his arms as he yawned. "I told you about that Russian kid, right?" he asked. "The one the feds bagged outside the house on Long Island, Victor something or other? He's out."

Greene was surprised. "You got to be kidding me," he said. "Wasn't he Singleton's cellmate? I thought the feds had them wrapped up forever."

"Legal bullshit," Pavlik said. "Some big-shot comrade from the Seagate crew hired an expensive lawyer to get Victor out for a few days. He was the victim of circumstances or some shit. He gets surrendered back into custody on parole violation tomorrow morning."

Greene straightened in his chair. "He knows where the missing bounty is," he said with a smile.

"Or why else would the Seagate crew give a fuck about him?" Pavlik asked back, smiling himself then. "His cousin was the guy Eddie Senta killed in the bedroom. He was a member of that crew. He must've told somebody something about what he was doing."

Greene was squinting. "And what about Murphy? Where's he in all this?"

Pavlik glanced down at the stain again. "Phalen's had his hooks into Murphy going on forever," he said. "They're like family. Murphy processes the handoffs from the feds to NYPD. The Russian's paperwork had to cross Murphy's desk."

"And you know all this how?"

"Think about it."

Greene leaned forward. "I know it wasn't Murphy told you," he said. "Phalen?"

Pavlik mocked the Irish brogue again. "Good God, boy-oh, I'm dating the man's sister."

"That a yes or a no?" Greene asked.

* * * * *

Peter Phalen pointed to the night-vision glasses that Detective William Murphy was holding on his lap. "I see you brought your secret X ray glasses," he said.

"I could guess," Murphy said. "But then you wouldn't really need me, would you?"

Both men were sitting in Phalen's Grand Marquis in an abandoned gas station on a service road alongside the Belt Parkway. Phalen was wearing black. A handheld radio was wedged upright between his legs. Murphy, a fifty-year-old stout man with reddish-gray hair, pale skin, and freckles, was wearing a charcoal gray sports jacket and matching slacks. He had just come from a funeral.

Phalen pointed at a dark car pulling into the motel parking lot that they were watching. "That him?" he asked Murphy.

Murphy leaned forward as he held the night-vision glasses against his eyes. "I think so," he said. "He's got company if it is him. Let's see when they get out."

The car that they were watching parked near the motel office. The driver, a short man with blond hair, got out of the car. He looked around and headed for the office. The other man remained in the car.

"That's your man," Murphy said. "The one went inside the office."

"You know the other one?" Phalen asked, as he grabbed the hand-held radio.

Murphy opened his hands. "Could be anybody," he said. "They couldn't let him come alone."

Phalen continued to watch the motel office door as he spoke into the radio. Two of his men were parked in a van around the corner from the motel. "On my signal," he told them.

Murphy was holding the night-vision glasses to his eyes again. The short man emerged from the office and waved to the man in the car. The tall, broad man got out of the car and followed the short man along the row of rooms that lined the parking lot.

"There they go," Murphy said.

Phalen watched intently until both men stopped at a room at the far end of the motel. The short man used a key to open the door. Both men entered the room. The door closed behind them, and Phalen turned to Murphy.

"Give me a room number," he said.

Murphy used his glasses one more time. "One-nineteen," he said. "Next to last room."

Phalen spoke into the radio. "Now," he said. "Take them. Next to last room. One-nineteen."

"This should be interesting," Murphy said.

"Shouldn't you be leaving about now?" Phalen asked. He handed Murphy a thick envelope.

Murphy slid the envelope inside of his jacket and nudged Phalen. "Your sister really seeing that homicide Polack works Manhattan?" he asked.

"As we speak," Phalen said without moving his eyes from the door at the far end of the parking lot.

"You should be ashamed of yourself," Murphy said.

Phalen saluted Murphy without moving his head. "Sweet dreams," he said.

Murphy walked around the corner to his own car and immediately left the area. Phalen lit a cigarette and watched the action unfold.

The van with Phalen's men pulled into the motel lot and blocked the exit. The doors of the van opened, and two men brandishing automatic weapons hugged the building as they headed for the far end of the motel.

Phalen opened his window to let smoke escape. He glanced at all three car mirrors before he turned his attention to the motel again. Phalen's men were standing in front of room one-nineteen. The bigger of the two kicked the door open. Both went inside with their weapons showing. Phalen glanced at his watch a split second before two quick flashes filled the room's windows. The delayed pops of the muffled shots were barely audible against the noise of eastbound cars pushing the speed limit on the Belt Parkway. Another two muffled gunshots followed a few seconds later. Less than a minute passed before both men left the room. One of them carried a black bag.

CHAPTER 39

"The waiting sucks," Jack Senta said.

Eddie waved at his son to come closer. "Sometimes it's the worst part," he said.

They were sitting in Eddie's lawyer's office waiting for the final terms of a plea agreement with the Nassau County District Attorney. The room that they were waiting in was a huge wood-paneled conference room overlooking Battery Park. The Statue of Liberty was visible in the distance.

Jack Senta rolled his wheelchair alongside his father. He fidgeted with the robe that he wore to hide his bandage. "I'm glad you have this lawyer," he said. "I've seen him in the papers. I know he's a big shot."

Eddie smirked. "My last favor, and I didn't even ask this time."

"Huh?" Jack said.

Eddie shook his head.

"What if it's two years?" he asked.

Eddie furrowed his eyebrows. "Then it's two years. Tommy's dead, Jack. Some other people, too. They don't get to come back."

"But those guys were going to kill us," Jack said. "Diane and me. She held on to me as long as she could, Dad. She didn't want to let me go."

"It's not about those guys," Eddie told his son. He moved the ashtray to his lap and crushed out his cigarette. "It's complicated, Jack. Probably none of this will ever make any sense. No matter how it works out. I'm just lucky is all. No matter what happens, I have to consider myself lucky."

Jack was struggling with his father's explanation. "But gun possession? How were you supposed to kill those guys?"

Eddie half-smiled. "Gun possession is a blessing right now," he said. "Someday you'll understand that part better. This all happened because of a decision I made a month or so ago. It was all avoidable."

Jack shook his head. "I don't see where you did anything wrong," he said. "You did what you had to do."

"No," Eddie said. "I didn't have to do any of this. Ever. It was my choice. It's not so unlike cutting woodshop. That was a bad choice. You had to write an opera paper. My choice was dangerous. It was stupid. Now I have to pay for it. I'm lucky enough to be alive. I'm lucky nothing more serious happened to you."

"Or Diane," Jack added.

Eddie bit his upper lip as he took his son's right hand. "Yeah, Diane, too," he said. "I'm lucky nothing happened to her, either."

One of the two doors to the conference room opened. A large bald man in a dark-gray suit stepped inside. Diane followed him, sobbing.

The bald man removed the gold-framed glasses that he was wearing and put a hand on Eddie's right shoulder as he sat at the head of the conference table.

"Six months, Nassau House of Detention," the bald man said. "A cakewalk. You'll be out for Christmas." He pointed from Jack to his father. "The two of you will be riding Christmas bikes together."

Diane took the seat beside Eddie. She immediately took his right hand.

Eddie swallowed hard. He turned to Jack. Jack looked scared.

"That's not so bad, Jack," Eddie said.

Jack turned pale.

"Nassau isn't nearly as bad as Riker's Island," the bald man said. "It's not federal, so you won't be playing tennis, but it isn't a zoo like Riker's either. But it's still jail. Make no mistake. None of us can do anything about that. My guy in Nassau got you a great deal. It'll go fast enough. You have skills you can actually use in there. Teaching other inmates. My guy said that word processing job you have was a good sell."

"How are you at Internet sex?" Eddie asked in a whisper to his wife. "If they let me go on-line and chat."

Diane leaned into Eddie's shoulder. She continued to sob.

"When do I start?" Eddie asked the bald man.

"Three days. You surrender on the fourteenth. I can get you a day or two extension if you need it, but no more than that."

Eddie took a deep breath. "Let's get it over with," he said.

"Can he get out early?" Diane asked. "For good behavior?"

The bald man frowned at Eddie. "You understand how these things work, right?"

Eddie crushed his cigarette again.

"The gun possession was a trade off," the bald man told Diane. "The New York D.A. wanted the homicide-burglary more thoroughly investigated, but my guess is the Federal government didn't. Nobody is even asking questions about the money or the gold coins. Nobody cares. All the New York D.A. really had was your friend's wife, but that was easy enough to squash. She originally told the police exactly what you told me. It was a burglary they couldn't hang on you."

"Except Tommy is dead," Eddie said.

"Missing," the bald man said, correcting Eddie.

Eddie smirked. "What about the feds?" he asked. "Is there any-thing down the road with them?"

The bald man waved off the question. "They screwed up big time," he said. "They're very content running for cover on this one. They still have Singleton's testimony on some drug dealer in Brooklyn, which is more than they had if Singleton died. The last thing they want is the publicity of a trial. I'm sure they helped convince the D.A. a trial wasn't a good thing."

"And the Russian mob?" Eddie asked. "Do I have anything to worry about with them?"

"Not according to Organized Crime intelligence," the bald man said. "The Russians aren't eager to provoke the Federal Department of Justice just yet. The guy you killed took a big risk and lost. Organized Crime claims the Russians will handle their own dirty laundry without bringing attention to themselves. It was bad publicity for them, too, what that Russian did."

"And nothing else happens to Singleton," Eddie said. "Not for Sarah or anybody."

The bald man rubbed his forehead. "He's in the program," he said. "He'll get to work on his forehand down south someplace after he tes-tifies. He already has the tan."

"Is that it?" Diane asked. "For killing three people?"

"Well, he didn't exactly confess to that," the bald man said. "And like I said, the feds don't want this at trial. They aren't fond of airing their dirty laundry like that. I guess their friend Sammy the Snitch keeps them looking bad enough. Especially since he's gone back into the construction and drug-dealing businesses compliments of the Fed-eral government. You believe that? The guy gets a freebee new start life after admitting he killed a couple dozen people, they move him out to the desert someplace, and he starts selling drugs. I wonder if the jury that convicted Mr. Gotti feels foolish now?"

Eddie continued to crush his cigarette. "I guess that puts things back in order, huh? The government gets some drug dealer."

"A nickel and dimer, too," the bald man said. "They get him with the expectation he gives up somebody else."

"And then he makes a deal, too," Eddie said.

The bald man shrugged.

"It's so unfair," Diane said.

"You did take one of his eyes out," the bald man told Eddie. "If it's any conciliation. Half the bone under his eye socket, too. From what I hear, he looks like a monster. He'll be in and out of plastic surgery the rest of his life, however long that is."

The bald man fidgeted with a cigarette from his gold case. "Why don't the two of you sell your house," he said. "Prices are good in Port Washington right now. I'm in Manhasset myself. It'll give you something to focus on while Eddie is away."

Eddie tilted his head at Diane. "Might be a good idea," he said.

Diane ignored the question. "What about after he's through testifying?" she asked. "This Singleton, won't he come looking for Eddie?"

The bald man leaned both arms on his desk. "Sell the house," he said. "Really, prices are good."